Clarice Bean
Spells Trouble

Copyright © 2004 by Lauren Child

First U.S. paperback edition 2006

First published in Great Britain in 2004 by Orchard Books, London

The Library of Congress has cataloged the hardcover edition as follows:

Child, Lauren.
Clarice Bean spells trouble / Lauren Child. —1st U.S. ed.
p. cm.
Summary: Clarice Bean, aspiring actress and author, unsuccessfully
tries to avoid getting into trouble as she attempts to help a friend in
need by following the rules of the fictional spy Ruby Redfort.
ISBN 978-0-7636-2813-0 (hardcover)
[1. Conduct of life—Fiction. 2. Friendship—Fiction. 3. Authorship—Fiction. 4. Schools—
Fiction. 5. Family life—Fiction. 6. Humorous stories.] I. Title.
PZ7.C4383Cku 2005
[Fic]—dc22   2005045787

ISBN 978-0-7636-2903-8 (paperback)

11 12 13 14 15 16 WOR 18 17 16 15 14 13

Printed in Stevens Point, WI, U.S.A.

This book was typeset in M Bembo.

Candlewick Press
99 Dover Street
Somerville, Massachusetts 02144

visit us at www.candlewick.com

Clarice Bean
Spells
Trouble

Lauren Child

CANDLEWICK PRESS

Things
you can't Explain—like
why isn't YOU
spelled U?

You might want to know why I did what I did.
  But if you were me, you would understand that
sometimes I just don't know why I do things.
  So it's hard to explain.
  I just get this urge to do something and I do it.
  And before I know it,
    I am in very big trouble.
  My mom is always telling me I must think before
I open my mouth and then perhaps life would be a
lot easier.
  She is probably right.
  But try telling my brain that;
    it doesn't think as fast as me.

Another thing that is difficult to explain is
      why YOU *isn't spelled* U
      and why WHY *isn't spelled* Y.
Spelling. Who knows where it all came from and why it has to be so difficult. Whoever thought it up must be a very strange person.

You see, it all started with this spelling bee that my teacher, Mrs. Wilberton, organized. It's to see who is the best out of all the spellers.

I am not a good speller; my mind just doesn't have the room in it to remember spellings.

It isn't my fault; it really isn't.

Think of all the other things in your whole life that you want to remember. Like that joke my brother Kurt told me once about the cow on the telephone.

And one time when we went on vacation and it rained like mad and we all got soaked through to our underwear, including everyone.

So spellings are not that important to me.

Compared to these other things,
      which are.

Anyway, what I am telling you is,
      spelling causes trouble.

For example, the thing that everyone said I did, the thing that got me into some very big trouble, mainly happened because of spelling.

Someone who is a good speller but is in nonstop trouble is Karl Wrenbury.

Karl Wrenbury is this boy in my class.

You have probably heard of him—most people have. He gets up to no good, but I don't think it's his fault really.

He has just got this zingy thing in him.

He can't control it.

And sometimes he lets the guinea pigs out
        on purpose.

I like Karl Wrenbury.

At first I didn't and then I got to know him,
        and then I did.

But he is the naughtiest person in the school, and the problem with knowing the naughtiest person is that then people think you are just as bad.

Why even try to be good?

This is something I have been finding out for myself at home.

My younger brother, Minal, has the knack of learning from my mistakes and avoiding trouble.

This mainly works by getting me into trouble.

I feel like I am turning into Karl Wrenbury.

I am in nonstop TROUBLE these days, which isn't fair, of course.

What happens is, Minal always goes something like "Mo-o-om, Clarice just *really pinched* me on the elbow!"

And of course this is utterly not true—

and if it is, it was for a very good reason.

And Mom says, "I am too busy and I have too big a headache to be dealing with two unpleasant children.

Either continue this argument on another planet or keep out of each other's way."

She isn't always like this—just when she has "had it up to here!"

Which lately she has.

My dad is different. He likes to sort things out.

He is good at that. It's part of his job and he has to do it every day at work.

Dad will not have squabbling.

Absolutely not.

He says, "You can agree to disagree by all means, you can discuss it, or you can change the subject."

But what my dad says you may not do is have two squealy voices driving him utterly around the bend.

Someone who is easily driven around the bend is my older sister, Marcie—she spends most of her time being crabby, and when she isn't being crabby, she is in the bathroom talking on the phone.

My brother Kurt is the oldest out of all of us, and he is mainly in his room not talking to anybody.

* * *

So now if you still don't understand why it's hard for someone like me to avoid trouble, you should try having Mrs. Wilberton as your teacher. Because if you are in Mrs. Wilberton's class and you are named Clarice Bean, you might as well face it: trouble is your middle name.

It's just how the cookie gets crumbled.

And I tell you, no one has ever gotten in more trouble in Mrs. Wilberton's class than I did last spring.

Who Decides what's **Important** and What **Isn't?**

Tuesday is not my favorite day because there is testing to see how smart everyone is and how can you see that in a test?

That's the thing about school: they might only test you for one thing, i.e.,

math

or spellingy type things

or punctuationy thingummybobs,

and they will not see that maybe you will know absolutely every episode of the Ruby Redfort series by heart. And that you can tell them how Ruby managed to jump out of a moving helicopter without twisting an ankle.

Which is a hard thing to do.

And maybe you will know how to cleverly mend
your hem with a stapler or stand on
your actual head—or stand on
your actual head while
drawing a dog in
ballpoint pen—or
teach your *dog* how
to draw with a ballpoint pen
while *he* stands on *your* head.

dog in
pen

But they do not test you for
these things because the people
who come up with the testing
do not think it is important.

But would you rather know someone who
knows how to jump out of a moving helicopter
without getting a twisted ankle or someone who
can spell *grapefruit*?

I would like to know someone who knows how
to get green marker out of a white carpet.

Until I do, Betty says put a chair on it.

I just hope my mom doesn't move the chairs
before I discover the answer.

Anyway, testing is my worst, whereas someone

like Grace Grapello, for an actual example, is good in a test situation because ask her what 3.3 divided by 2.4 ※ is and she will get a big check mark and I will get a headache.

Anyway, there we are doing this testing thing and the room is all quiet and I can just hear the clock ticking really slowly, but strangely, every minute I look up, it is ten minutes later and time is running out.

And I can hear Robert Granger breathing. That's what he does. He sits behind me and breathes. It drives me utterly crazy.

And I turn around and go, "Stop breathing, will you!"

And he says, "Clarice Bean, of course I cannot stop breathing because then I would be dead and how would you like that?"

I decide not to answer his question because Mom has taught me if you can't think of anything nice to say, then sometimes it is better to say nothing at all. You see, I am trying really hard to keep it zipped in class and I don't even utter a

※ $3.3 \div 2.4 = 1.375$

single word when I hear Grace Grapello telling
Cindy Fisher that I am a duh-brain because I
spelled PHOTO with an **F**.

Mrs. Wilberton didn't tell her *off* even; she just
said, "Clarice Bean, your spelling leaves a lot to
be desired."

Anyway, at the end, when time is up,

I hand in my test and

Mrs. Wilberton says,

"Oh deary dear,
it looks as if a spider has been
dipped in ink and struggled
across the page!"

I wish someone would dip *her* in ink.
Then she says, "I have some exciting news.
I have arranged for the whole school to
take part in a spelling bee."

Spelling bee * is just a fancy
way of saying *test,* but you have
to stand there in front of the whole
school and spell words out loud on
the spot without writing them down. It is
interesting that for Mrs. Wilberton, giving a
spelling test is the most fun she can ever have and
for me it is a very good reason to tell Mrs. Marse,
the school secretary, that I have a terrible case of a
tummy upset and I need to go home as soon as
possible, on the double, don't even bother to call
my mom.

Anyway, I have been wondering, who is the
person who gets to decide what is important?

Because I wish it was me.

* * *

In the playground, Karl Wrenbury is throwing
water balloons at Toby Hawkling. He gets Grace
Grapello by accident and she goes off to tell.

---

 * **Bee** (as in *spelling bee*) means lots of people all working on the same
thing at once, like bees all making honey together.

She is mad because he has gotten her rain jacket all wet, even though this is what rain jackets are for.

But that's Grace Grapello for you.

She is someone who I don't get along with because she is a know-it-all and a meany and her favorite thing is to tell on people.

I am trying really hard not to get in her way because I don't want to get in a tussle with Mrs. Wilberton and the thing is, Mrs. Wilberton always believes Grace and not me.

But after school I am collecting my coat from my peg and so is Karl and he is telling me a joke about a pig who crosses the road and before he can tell the last bit of it, the actual funny bit, Mrs. Wilberton walks by and says, "Now, move along, you two, before you get into mischief."

You see, Karl gets in trouble even when he is being well behaved.

This is one of the side effects of bad behavior.

I say, "We were just getting our coats on, Mrs. Wilberton."

And she says, "No answering back thank you very much."

I say, "Excuse me for breathing," but I say it really really quietly.

✷ ✷ ✷

I go home in a very downcast-ish mood, and even my older brother, Kurt, says, "What's the matter with you?"

Which is unusual because usually he doesn't notice other people's gloom—he is too busy feeling gloom himself.

When I ask Mom why he's so cheerful, she says, "He's just got himself this weekend job at Eggplant and it has really put him in a good mood."

 Eggplant is the local vegetarians' shop. Kurt himself is a vegetarian so he feels happy being surrounded by vegetables all day.

The only thing that can cheer me up is that Ruby Redfort is on TV tonight. I am utterly crazy about the Ruby Redfort books, as you may know, but unfortunately I am still waiting for Patricia F. Maplin Stacey to write a new one since I have read all the others at least maybe three times.

What's lucky is—and maybe you did not know this—but they are now televised for the TV and they are on twice a week.

There are loads of episodes, loads.

But it is not a new thing, the TV series. Mom says it was on in her day and they were made years ago, which is why the fashion looks a bit out of fashion.

They are reshowing it because Patricia F. Maplin Stacey has started writing books again and I'm sure they will be as popular as ever.

I didn't know all this information, but Betty looked it up on the Ruby Redfort website and told me. The new books will be quite different from the old ones and, I should think, more moderner.

Betty said, "Did you know she started writing the Ruby Redfort books way back, years and years ago in 1972?"—which was before most people were born.

The most exciting thing is that they are going to make Ruby Redfort into a movie.

Made by

HOLLYWOOD

Ruby is now thirteen and has this butler named Hitch who wears a suit and is in the know about all her secret-agent work. He is very handsome and good-looking—my mom is quite sweet on him.

Ruby has a best friend named Clancy Crew who is a boy who is very clever and also funny. They ride around together on bikes.

Me and Betty know all the Ruby phrases—she says things like, "Give me a break, bozo" and "Do you actually have a brain?"

You would be amazed if you know about Ruby Redfort because the Hollywood people will have to do all these gadgets and stuff. I am not sure how they will make them.

How do you make a walkie-talkie watch?

And roller skates that know which direction to go in if you say "Follow that car"?

And a purple helicopter that is bigger on the inside than on the outside?

The Ruby in the movie will be different from the one on the TV because the TV Ruby is now about almost at least 40 years old, if not more.

She is named Jodie O'Neal and she is utterly brilliant even though she has blond hair when she is meant to have brown.

I bet Jodie O'Neal never had to worry about being good in a spelling bee.

❋ ❋ ❋

I am lying in bed thinking about all this and I am staring at my poster Dad got me. It is of a rhinoceros and it says RHINOCEROS on it. I stare at this poster every night and it occurs to me now what a strange word the word *rhinoceros* is and how odd it is that it has an **H** in it when you wouldn't expect it to. You can't hear it in the word or anything.

I fall asleep and I dream that a rhinoceros charges into our school and eats Mrs. Wilberton. And he takes over the teaching and he turns out to be really good at math.

Strange what you think of when you aren't thinking about anything.

RHINOCEROS

Where does **Natural Talent** come from and **Why** do **some** people get **More** of it than **others?**

I wake up still thinking about Ruby Redfort becoming a movie and how exciting it will be. And how I wish I could be a child star because then I would miss the spelling bee.

I am really daydreaming about it and how when we have our school play, which is soon, I might get spotted by one of those people who spot children for being talents.

Since you see, what happens is every year my school puts on a play, which is a very important occasion and simply everyone comes.

This year it is *my* class who will be putting it on so it is a really good chance to be spotted.

I think I am a good actor and I like acting and I

could end up being in the movies, although I would quite like to run a cake shop.

I think about this all the way to school, but at school all my daydreaming vanishes and it is more dreariness because Mrs. Wilberton says, "I have a date for the school spelling bee and it will be the last Tuesday of school before summer vacation! So everybody, we have just a matter of weeks until the big day! So let's brush up our vocab and get spelling! Make sure you all have a dictionary at home—if you don't, you may borrow a school one. I want everyone to go through it learning as many spellings as they possibly can."

She must be crazy because there are at least a trillion words in the dictionary and the chances of me getting one of the ones I have learned coming up in the spelling bee are very minuscule if not less than minute. ✷

When the bell rings Mrs. Wilberton says, "Remember, only a few weeks to go before the big day!"

✷ **Minute** (sounds like *my-newt*), meaning very minuscule indeed, not *min-it* as in 60 seconds.

She says it as if this is a good thing and we should all be absolutely over the moon about it but I feel sick inside and Betty gives me that "What can you do?" look and I make an "I just don't know" face.

Betty Moody is my utterly best friend and she knows I am not a good speller and that it is not my fault if I don't know how many Z's there are in LOSER.

❈ ❈ ❈

After school Betty's mom and dad are there to pick her up because they are taking her to get some new glasses because their dog Ralph chewed the old ones. We tell them about the spelling bee.

Mrs. Moody-Call-Me-Mol says that she is not really big on spelling bees. She says, "Some people just have a brain for spelling and some people don't and some people's brains

s c r a m b l e

all the letters up so they just can't see them as words at all."

She says, "I shouldn't worry too much, Clarice. Spelling isn't the be-all and end-all, you know." And Mol is a writer so she should know.

Mr. Moody-Call-Me-Cecil says, "Yes, way back in the olden days, people used to spell words all kinds of different ways. Spelling wasn't as important as it is these days."

I say, "I wish it was the olden days now."

And Cecil and Mol laugh but I am not joking.

I say goodbye to them and start walking home. It's got me thinking: if spelling isn't my natural talent, then why haven't I got another one?

You see, there is something called natural talent and everybody has some of it, somewhere. Even if your natural talent is taking the lids off jars, which is what my uncle Ted is good at. Although this is 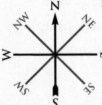 not his only talent—he is also good at knowing what direction to go in.

He just knows.

This is good because my uncle Ted is a firefighter and firefighters need to know where they are going in a hurry.

Karl Wrenbury's natural talent is dog training. He just has the knack of it.

He may have learned it from his mom because his mom is a professional—she does dog training as a living and also dog walking. He says, "You have to talk to dogs as if you yourself are a dog." He says, "Most people don't agree with that, but it works for me. If you treat them like you are in a pack of wolves but you are the main in-charge wolf, you will be their top dog and all the dogs will look up to you." He says he does it by HOWLING.

Karl says, "The most important thing to train a dog with is manners. But you have to be careful because you do not want to break their spirit by being too strict because then a dog is no fun."

It's the same with human beings. You want them to have manners but at the same time not be too boring.

Robert Granger is a perfect example of this going wrong, and in fact his manners are not that good either, unless it is good manners to stick your finger up your nose while you are talking to somebody.

We have got a very rudish dog at home. He has simply got no manners—he learned that from Grandad.

Grandad has actually got manners but he doesn't use them that much anymore and he hasn't let the dog see them, which is why Cement is utterly mannerless. I am going to take him to dog training with Karl because Mom says things have got to change around here and we might as well start with the dog.

I am thinking about all this while I am walking past the shop where Kurt has started working called Eggplant. Another word for *eggplant* is *aubergine*. Except *aubergine* is foreign or French for it. It's the same thing with zucchini—they have another name too, which I can't quite remember but it sounds a bit like the car Corvette. ✳

✳ **courgette**

My mom says *aubergine* and my dad says *eggplant* but it's the same. You can say either. I do.

Eggplant is an organic shop as well as being vegetarian. It's all about selling things that haven't been sprayed with chemically things.

I am not sure what that word *organic* exactly stands for really. Who does know? They should call it "with bugs" or something so people know what they are in for. You might find a caterpillar in your broccoli but that's the point.

Mom says, "There's nothing wrong with eating a caterpillar."

I say, "There is if you are vegetarian."

Anyway, today I am walking past when I see this notice taped to the window. It says,

> ## Express yourself with drama.
> ### Why not join the children's drama, dance, and voice workshop?
>
> For more information call
> Czarina at 555-2667.

Luckily I have my Ruby Redfort secret-agent pen and so can quickly scribble down the number on my arm. It starts off invisible and you can only see it when you rub it.

When I get in, I tell Mom about the drama, dance workshop thingy and I ask her if I can join and Mom says, "Anything that means less time arguing with your brother will be fine with me." She means my younger brother, Minal, who is an earwig.

I really very much want to join up as soon as possible, so once I have finished my spaghetti, I call Betty Moody. I say, "Would you like me to put your name down for the new drama workshop?"

And Betty says, "Sure."

I call the Czarina number and I just get an answery phoney type of message. It has sort of music, which is sort of not like music and more like water and a pipeish type of a noise.

The voice says,
*"Never lose sight of your **dreams** — act on them. For information about the **drama** workshops, please leave your name and number after the tone. And remember to have an **interesting** day."*

I leave my message and I hope I will not forget to have an interesting day. And I wonder to myself if maybe drama might be my natural talent.

You might just as well be **Bad** all the time

Three nice things happened today.

One was that I got a package. It was from my granny. She sometimes just mails things off to us when she sees something that we might like. It doesn't have to be our birthday or anything.

There is a note, which says, "I thought you would love this." And when I unwrap it, I really totally do.

It's a Ruby Redfort notebook with a padlock. No one can read anything you write unless they have the key. But you wear the key on a special secret necklace, so nosy parkers will never find it.

And they don't even know that it is a secret Ruby Redfort notebook because it doesn't say

Ruby Redfort on the front. It just has a fly on
the cover, which disappears when
you tip it.

It's a typical thing Ruby Redfort does—i.e., not draw attention to her secret ideas.

Inside, it has all these Ruby Redfort Rules and useful facts and things—things like how to survive an emergency.

Or what to do if you are being tailed by an arch villain.

Or how to fake being asleep in a realistical way.

It's got all these good tips and clever advice. Like Ruby's rule of NEVER GET ON ANYONE'S BAD SIDE IF YOU WANT SOMETHING FROM THEM. It sounds like a simple rule, but it's surprising how many times one can forget this.

I decide that I am going to use my Ruby Redfort notebook to write down all sorts of suspicious things I see and interesting things I overhear by accident.

Even Betty Moody doesn't have one of these. And when I get to school, she says, "Wow, Clarice Bean, you are lucky!"

❋ ❋ ❋

Then, the second good thing which happens is,

Betty gives me a badge that she has made on her badge-maker machine. It says **CB** on it in red printing. It stands for *Clarice Bean,* of course. Betty has one that says **BP**, which stands for *Betty P.* P. is Betty's middle name—it's just a letter, not a word. She made it up herself.

You probably know she got the idea for badges from Ruby Redfort, who has a badge on her pants with **RR** on. And her friend Clancy Crew has one with **CC** on. Hitch doesn't wear a badge because he has a suit and it wouldn't look right with a badge on it.

❋ ❋ ❋

The third good thing that happened is, there's this teacher who's arrived at our school. He is from Trinidad on exchange.

We have sent *them*—Mr. Fellows.

Why people do exchanges is to learn what it's like to do the same thing that you normally do but in a different place.

My older sister, Marcie, is on an exchange at the moment in France. What she is learning is French.

And what *I* am learning is, you are much more likely to get a turn in the bathroom if your older sister is in France.

Anyway, our exchange teacher person is named Mr. something—I'm not sure what. He wears sneakers. Everyone is talking about him.

And some people are going to get him as their teacher, just for a few weeks.

Betty and me see him in the corridor and we go up to him and we say, "Sir, we like your T-shirt" because it has a picture of a swimming dog on it.

And I say, "It is exceptionordinarily nice."

And he says, "Thanks, **CB** and **BP**."

Which is really funny.

We say, "What is your name, sir?"

And he says, "**PW**, but you can call me Mr. Washington."

We can tell he is a very funny person.

He has a different kind of accent because he is from Trinidad, which is in the Caribbean, which is where my aunt named Marguerite was from before she met Mom's brother, Uncle Al, and they had my cousins Yolla and Noah. And now they live around the corner.

And Grandad's favorite sports player is from Trinidad.

I hope we get Mr. Washington as our teacher. He seems really nice.

I draw a picture of the picture on his T-shirt in my Ruby notebook because it's the kind of thing that interests me.

Stay Cool

✳ ✳ ✳

After lunch Mrs. Wilberton says, "Mrs. Greenford and I will be conducting auditions for the school play. They will be taking place during lunch break, and anyone who wants a main part must come along. I will not be revealing what the play will be until afterward because we do not want any silly showing off."

I am really utterly excited and I am hoping for a good part this time.

Last year I was a carrot.

I had two lines.

And one of them was, "I am a carrot."

I have no interest in playing a speaking vegetable. It's not realistic.

I don't mind people using their imaginations to come up with strange and unusual things but this is not interesting because who wants to know what a carrot would say if it could talk?

The answer is no one, that's who, because a carrot has spent its whole life underground, in the dark, growing into a carrot.

And then it gets picked—so it has nothing to say for itself. It has not had an interesting life. Even if it has met a worm.

Anyway, me and Betty Moody are very excited to know just what the play will turn out to be. We are hoping it will not be one Mrs. Wilberton has written. She is completely crazy about dance. So absolutely everything has to end up dancing even if it is a cheese or a wasp.

The auditions turn out to be really stupid.

We have to do things like pretend we are
trees growing in a forest and then hop
around like squirrels and things that have got
nothing to do with acting as far as I can see. And
I am just standing there minding my own business,
trying to be a stupid squirrel, and Mrs. Wilberton
tells me off for absolutely no reason at all. It is
utterly dreary and not at all fun in any way.

When I get home from school, Minal runs into
the kitchen and bumps into the table and knocks
over a glass of water and Mom says, "Do you
think you two could go and run around in the
yard until you have calmed down, please."

And I say, "I wasn't even calmed up."

And she says, "It's been a long and tiring day,
and I am just not in the mood for silliness."

You see what I mean—you might just as well
be bad all the time.

Because you get in trouble for it anyway.

Some days start off **Bad** and End up really **Good**

4

Today Karl wrote something on the school notice board, which as it turned out was not such a good idea.

Although it does prove that he is a good speller.

But if you are going to write,

Mrs. Wilberton has trotters

then don't do it while she is walking along the corridor. ✳

He said it wasn't him. Which was also not a good idea, since then Mrs. Wilberton said, "Well, Karl Wrenbury, you must either think I am blind or that I am very stupid indeed."

And Karl said, "Well, I know you aren't blind."

✳ **Trotters**—pig's feet

Mrs. Wilberton said she will need the weekend to think of a fitting punishment as she has run out of all the good ones.

* * *

Because I am exceptionordinarily eager to be in the school play and I do want a main part, I decide I must get on Mrs. Wilberton's good side and keep out of trouble.

Ruby Redfort would call it KEEPING A LOW PROFILE, I.E., DON'T DRAW ATTENTION TO YOURSELF. BLEND IN WITH EVERYONE ELSE AND TRY TO DO WHAT THEY ARE DOING. It's a Ruby Redfort rule.

So I look across the room to see what everyone else *is* doing and I catch sight of Robert Granger sticking a pencil up his nose and leaving it there.

I decide not to blend in with him.

Instead I copy Grace Grapello since she is one of Mrs. Wilberton's favorites. But it turns out to be very difficult to do her smug goody-two-shoes smile, so instead I make up my own blending-in face.

And so there I am, sitting with lots of concentration showing on my face. I do this by slightly crinkling my eyebrows so she can see, anyone could, that I am listening and most probably learning too, even though it is highly dreary, what she is saying.

It doesn't seem to work, though, and before even about 4ish minutes I suddenly hear this honking voice going, "Clarice Bean, I know what you are thinking. I can see by the look on your face, you are up to no good."

And I want to say, "Even I don't know what I am thinking because I have gone off in a trance of boredom and actually for your information, I wasn't thinking at all." But then she would just say, "I knew it! Wasting time, staring into space, vacant mind. Well, obviously you need to fill that empty brain up with the eight times table."

So instead I say, "But Mrs. Wilberton, I am finding your lesson exceptionordinarily interesting and I am just concentrating hard on being fascinated by the interesting things you are saying."

And Mrs. Wilberton says,

"For a start, I find that very hard to believe, and second, there is no such word as

exceptionordinarily—you're making it up, and you can't just make up words willy-nilly, you know.

Where would we be if we all just
made up words?"

So you see, I can't win. So I just have to sit there not saying a peep.

My mom is trying to train me not to answer back. She says, "Not answering back will save you a lot of time in the long run," and so, although I am tempted to say something, I don't, because I want a main part.

So I must keep zipped.

Ruby Redfort has a good technique for keeping it zipped, which is to put a couple of jawbreakers in her mouth, but there is a rule in our class of no gum chewing, so I can't use this brilliant idea.

By the way, for your information, the only actual person who can tell what I am thinking is my mother. She's really good at it. She says she has had plenty of experience, having been a mother for nearly half of her life. She says, "Mind reading is one of those things that mothers do really well." She says she's never really got the hang of the ironing, but mind reading, that's something she is really good at.

✻ ✻ ✻

In the afternoon, Mrs. Wilberton announces what the school play will be. It turns out we will be doing

THE SOUND OF MUSIC ♫♪

which Karl says is a drip's movie and there is no way he would ever be in it,
      which I agree about but secretly actually don't care. And am desperately eager to be in.
   You have probably seen the movie yourself

because I tell you it is on at least once during Christmastime. Grandad loves it, but Dad always offers to do the dishes as soon as it even starts.

He says he would rather sit with a rabid dog in a dark room for 3 hours than be made to watch **THE SOUND OF MUSIC.**

Betty says preferably she would like to play the leading part of Julie Andrews, who in the story is called Maria. Maria is a nun with a good voice who becomes a nanny and marries Captain von Trapp, who is a father of sevenish or so children. The children all end up wearing outfits made of a pair of curtains and turn out to be really good singers too.

I would rather very much like to be the eldest daughter of Captain von Trapp, named Liesl. Liesl has a boyfriend who turns into a Nazi, but before that he is a mailman.

Betty and me sometimes do the running down the hill in an apron when we are out in the park. I don't tell Karl that.

What does cheer me up after this dreary day at school is that Betty and me have got our first drama, dance, voice workshop.

We go along to the drama studio—it's the same place where Mom does her yoga classes and it stinks of these stick things they burn to cover up the smellings of feet.

We try to get Karl to come too, but he won't. He says he would rather be with his dog than doodle around pretending to be something he is not.

It's a shame because it turns out to be really fascinating and also interesting.

The teacher, Czarina, is from an actual drama teaching school of drama and she is madly attractive with an actual earring in her nose. She wears these kind of loose pajama-ry outfits and little tiny shoes a bit like dancing shoes but not. They have sequins on them.

She walks on tiptoe nearly always.

She is half from Pakistan. But her name is from Russia:

C . Z . A . R . I . N . A .

which you have to pronounce *za-rina,* so I don't
know why you have to bother with the **C** but
that's English for you.

Anyway Betty and me think Czarina is a very
glamorous name
even with an unneeded **C**
and we wish we were called it.

Czarina calls everyone "*My darlinks*" all the
time, whoever you are. And she says acting is a
craft, but it is not a bit like the crafts I am used to
doing, which are more about using felt and an odd
sort of glue that smells of fish.

She gets us to do all these special exercises
that she says actors are trained to do. You have
to do this special breathing and stretching and
say these rhymes that are really difficult to say
and you have to do them over and over
very fast.

Czarina says,
"*Darlinks, you must connect with the audience,
draw them in, make them love you, make them
hate you. Use your voice, your body, your energy.
Captivate them — don't let them go.*"

We have to do standing up straight and breathing deeply right from our ankles up.

Czarina says,

*"Fill your **whole** body with oxygen — feel it in your legs and tummy and fingers. Now float yourself across the floor. Are you floating, darlinks?"*

It's so exciting—I didn't think I could float, but when she says it like that, I feel like I can.

Czarina says,

*"You are all **fabulous, darlinks** — floating fabulousnesses."*

It is really amazing to find out I am good at something I thought I wasn't good at.

Czarina says,

*"Yes, it is **extraordinary** how **talent** creeps up on us when we are **least** expecting it."*

Wow! So Czarina thinks I am a talent.

Sometimes you Think you Know People and then you Realize you Don't

On Saturday Betty Moody comes over and Mom asks us if we will go to the vegetarians' shop to get some tofu, which looks a bit like a very palish cheese but tastes of nothing.

When we go into the shop, there are lots of girls all trying to get Kurt to serve them and we have to keep waving to get him to notice us.

Kurt is just becoming attractive—that's what Mom says, anyway. I can see what she means; he looks better than he used to. He has less acne and his hair knows what it's doing more.

Kurt has to wear this T-shirt with *Eggplant* written on it.

He's good at his job—he really seems to know what he is up to.

I am itching to have a job myself actually. I like the idea of working at the organic vegetarian shop because I like putting things in brown paper bags and twizzling them. Which is mainly what you have to do.

In the shop, lots of the girls are all giggling quite a lot and saying, "Oh, Kurt, you are funny." And Kurt *is* quite funny but not *that* funny. I am slightly funnier and no one is laughing at my jokes, not even Betty.

Waldo Park is in the shop too. He is the shop's owner, and Betty and me think his name sounds utterly like a movie star.

He is a very funny man and he is always joking around, but a lot of the customers don't get his jokes because Waldo Park is very good at keeping a straight face and not letting on that he is funny. Most of them just think he is a bit strange.

This customer comes in—she is always in Eggplant.

She wears flip-flops even in the winter.

Waldo Park says, "Hello, Sukie. How are you today?"

And she says, "Fine except I've got a sore bit in my armpit."

And Waldo Park says, "I think you'll find it's pronounced sorbet ※ and a damp cloth should remove it."

Do you get it? I don't.

Since it is impossible to get served by my brother, I have to ask Waldo Park for some of that bread that is very heavy and is made with too many seeds. My mom loves it, but Grandad and I find it very difficult to chew. The trick is you must drink lots of water.

Waldo Park says, "The shop is teeming with teens. I am beginning to feel a bit like a gooseberry. . . . Unfortunately I just sold the last ones." It's true, though—I have never seen so many customers who are girls around 14 to 17 years of age.

※ **Sorbet** (sounds like *sor-bay*) is an iced fruit dessert. If you say it wrong, i.e., *sor-bet*, it sounds a bit like *sore bit*.

Kurt doesn't seem to be noticing any of it, which is a bit what he can be like.

He is a Pisces. Or a Piscerian, which sounds like a vegetarian but is in fact a word for the kind of personality you are.

It all depends on which month you are born in, and if it is February, you might probably be the sign of a fish and you will probably be a bit dreamy and not be able to concentrate. I found that out from the horoscopes.

Mom says, "Kurt is a typical Pisces."

Which is true.

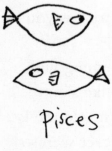

Pisces

He is a bit like a fish because he looks quite sad most of the time, which is what fish do, and he just wanders about not saying much, which is exactly what fish do.

My mother reads the horoscopes all the time, although she says she doesn't believe a word of it.

Someone drops a jar of organic pickles and the smell is not pleasant so Betty and me decide to make a quick getaway after we have bought some blue corn chips and a strange juice that smells of armpits slightly.

Then we go and sit on the bench outside.

Betty says she has been to the Ruby Redfort website again and there is much more information about the Hollywood filming and it has pictures of all the Hollywood actors who will be in it.

Apart from Ruby Redfort herself, the most important part is Hitch.

If you don't already know, Hitch is a really amazing man. He does all this secret-agent stuff for Ruby and everyone thinks he is just a butler. And he is—but not just.

He gets Ruby cups of tea in the morning but also drives her purple helicopter around rescuing her.

Betty says, "The new Hitch looks just exactly almost like the old one," i.e., tidy hair, all neat and slightly with a bit of gray. He has identicalish eyebrows to the last Hitch.

It's amazing what you can learn on the Internet. I don't get to go on it usually because Kurt has it in his room and Minal and me cannot be trusted.

When we have finished our snacks, we go along to watch Grandad and Cement being trained by Karl to have manners. They are in the park at the bottom of the hill.

I am expecting it to be quite dreary because we are not allowed to talk or interrupt and you would think being trained to have manners would be quite boring. But it turns out not to be.

Karl is really good at training, and Grandad and Cement learn it all quite fast. The main thing Karl is trying to do is stop Cement from jumping up on people and barking like a crazy dog. And the main thing he is trying to stop Grandad doing is encouraging Cement to.

I am really impressed by Karl, and he is really nice to Grandad. Even when he does something wrong, he always says, "Don't worry—you will get the hang of it."

And actually I think Karl would make a good teacher person. You can tell they both like him.

When Karl spots us, he does his impression of Mrs. Wilberton having trotters—which even Grandad thinks is exceptionordinarily funny and he's never even seen Mrs. Wilberton's trotter feet.

Afterward, Karl comes back to our house for supper. Mom makes us tofu burgers as an experiment, and they are a bit odd. But Karl is really polite and says they are interesting.

My mom says, "How's your mother, Karl? Is her dog-walking business going well?"

And Karl says, "She's OK. The dog walking is going really well and she does five at once usually but Mr. Patching's dog had to be put to sleep because it was very age-ed so she doesn't have that one anymore."

Mom says, "Well, do say hello from me—maybe I will see her at the school play."

And Karl says, "Maybe."

After supper, me, him, and Betty are talking about the new Hollywood movie of Ruby Redfort and how great it will be. I say, "I just don't know how they will show Ruby Redfort flying with her tiny glider wings."

Karl says, "It's easy—they do it all with special effects and little models and computers and stuff." Karl really knows about all that kind of thing.

Betty says, "They are going to do some of the filming here, and who knows, maybe near where we live."

Betty watched a program about movie stars and what happens is, when they are filming they live in trailers.

I say, "I wish I could live in a trailer."

Karl says, "I used to live in a trailer, before we moved here—before my dad left."

I say, "Wow, I didn't know that—how exciting."

Karl says, "It wasn't really. It was a bit leaky."

Karl's dad was a truck driver who then got out of work and was quite in the dumps about it. And anyway, he just went off and never came back and no one knows where he is.

And Karl keeps waiting for him to call. But he never does.

There's lots of stuff about Karl I don't know and there's lots of stuff he won't tell you. But everything he does tell you is usually really interesting.

Karl Wrenbury is a very private person.

You think you know him and then you realize you don't.

＊ *＊* *＊*

When Karl and Betty have gone, I ask Mom, "Why do you think Karl's dad has just gone off like he has, without keeping in contact, and will he ever come back, do you think?"

And Mom says, "Sometimes people just can't cope with life and they get in a muddle and it can be hard to see a way out."

And I say, "But why doesn't Karl's mom look for Mr. Wrenbury, because Karl really misses his dad, and why doesn't she want to find him for Karl?"

And Mom says, "I'm sure she has her reasons— perhaps she knows that Karl's dad can't be a dad at the moment. It doesn't mean he's a bad person. Things aren't always so simple."

I wish things *were* more simple, but this is something I am learning—it's very hard sometimes not to be in a muddle.

I go and flick on the TV. It's in the middle of an episode of Ruby Redfort called

TAKES ONE TO KNOW ONE.

It's all very exciting because Ruby Redfort has just received a dreadfully posh invitation to Marty Stanmore's party—he is a millionaire boy from Twinford. And he always has marvelous parties all the time.

Ruby is standing there looking at the invitation, and at that moment Clancy Crew comes skidding up to her on his bike.

He says, "Hey, have you heard about Marty Stanmore's party? Everyone's been invited—isn't it weird that we haven't?"

Then Ruby looks at the invitation. Then she looks at Clancy Crew, and that's when Ruby knows that Clancy is the only one who hasn't been invited. This is of course unfair because Marty Stanmore doesn't like Clancy Crew because he is so cool.

Anyway, Ruby doesn't want Clancy to know this because she knows this will upset him. And then at that minute Clancy spots the invitation and says, "But what's that in your hand?"

And Ruby Redfort thinks really fast and says, "What, this old thing? Just some new pizza delivery flier—doesn't look that good though—I sure won't be going." And then she puts it in the trash.

And the episode ends with Hitch taking Clancy Crew and Ruby Redfort off for a ride in the purple helicopter instead of going to Marty Stanmore's posh party. And right at the end of the program, Ruby says to Hitch,

"You know, **sometimes** it's better for people **not** to be in the know—if **what** they know ain't **good** to know."

I think I know what she means.

It is **Hard** to be **Happy** for your Best Friend when you are **Utterly Disappointed** yourself

On Monday, back at school, Karl Wrenbury is in one of his strange moods where he is on purposely causing himself to get told off.

He is not even being funny.

Just stupid.

He has been going around snapping people's pencils in half. ❋

When I say, "Why?"

He just says, "Why not?"

He says it in this annoying voice that he uses to make Toby Hawkling laugh.

No one else at all finds it funny.

It's easy to make Toby Hawkling laugh—you

❋ Sometimes it is a help to snap a pencil if you are feeling utterly stressed.

only have to say "bum" and sometimes not even that. I don't bother talking to Karl when he is like this.

Mrs. Wilberton is walking about in this very pleased-with-herself way and then she says, "When everybody is QUITE ready and has stopped talking, I have an announcement to make."

Of course she doesn't wait for everybody to be ready—she never does—so why does she bother saying it?

She says, "I am putting up a list of the people who will be in the school production. Everybody who wants to be in it will have a part of some sort, and that even includes Karl Wrenbury, who I know thinks he is above being in **THE SOUND OF MUSIC**, but I am afraid for *you*, Karl, it is compulsory." Which means he has to be in it, like it or not.

Being in the school play is his punishment for the notice about Mrs. Wilberton's legs looking like trotters.

I look at the list and find out I will not be playing

the part of Liesl von Trapp but will be nun four.

I am utterly disappointed. And I can't understand it because Czarina says I have a natural ability to express myself with drama.

And Czarina is a really good drama person. And if she says I am good and I have natural ability to express myself, then I am sure she is right.

So why am I playing *one of the nuns*?

I don't want to play *a* nun;

I want to wear a nice outfit.

I am only allowed to be a backup voice of singing because Mrs. Wilberton tells me that I do not have a good voice. She says it is loud without being tuneful. Which is not her paying me a compliment.

I always thought I was a good singer. Anyway, people who have a voice that sounds like a foghorn should be careful about telling other people they are not tuneful.

Of course Grace Grapello is going to play the part of Liesl, which she has only gotten because everyone thinks she is so pretty and is a good singer. And she does tap dancing.

1

Betty is going to play Louisa, which is the second main one of the von Trapp children. I am finding it quite tricky to be pleased for Betty *and* also say that I am pleased because I would adore to play the part of Louisa and I can barely utterly speak because I am very full of envy.

But Betty says, "Your part is important because you are one of the nuns who pushes Maria out into the big wide world and therefore why she meets Captain von Trapp and ends up falling in love with him and getting married and escaping from the Nazis and everything.

"And so really, when you think about it, to be playing 'one of the nuns' is the most important thing, whereas Louisa is just one

3   4   5   6   7

of the many von Trapp children and if she wasn't there, no one would even notice."

Suzie Woo will be Maria.

Karl hasn't bothered to look at the list. He says, "The only part that's any good is the Captain von Trapp one. If I have to be in a drippy play, I hope I get to be him." He wants to order everyone around, which is something that Captain von Trapp does quite a lot.

But Mrs. Wilberton says, "Karl is to play Rolf, who is the boyfriend of Liesl."

Karl says, "This is a sissy part!" and he will not be doing any kissing.

Captain von Trapp is being played by Robert Granger, which is of course ridiculous.

I do not think this will be a good school play in fact.

✳ ✳ ✳

I walk home from school on my own because Betty has to go off to her trumpet lesson.
Betty says she isn't enjoying learning the trumpet because she thinks her cheeks are stretching.

So far I am not learning an instrument, but I think I will soon because, who knows, I might be really good at it and if I don't try, I will never know and that might be my natural talent,
     musicalness.
And then I will have missed my chance to be really famous and well known as a household name. Which would be a shame.

Betty says she doesn't think she will be a household name for the trumpet.

Now it is more important than ever for me to find what my natural talent is, since I will not get to be spotted for my drama. Not being picked for things is a very scarring thing for a child—that's what Betty's mom, Mol, says.

I am absolutely covered in scars.

❋ ❋ ❋

When I get in, I go and watch one of my Ruby Redfort videos because I want to find out what Ruby would do in my situation, i.e., utterly disappointed.

It's an episode called

IT AIN'T SO BAD, RUBY.

It's all about Ruby getting sick so she can't take part in her school swimming competition, and of course she is the best swimmer and the team really needs her and she would have won the gold medal and been even more popular than usual, and you see, it all seems like a disaster for her and an utter shame.

But then because she is out of school at home sick and not even on a mission or anything it just happens that this really famous movie star named Baker Irving is whizzing past her house in his sports car and suddenly gets a flat and has to knock on Ruby's door to get help because it turns out he is not good with flats.

And nobody but Ruby is in because Hitch has had to drive her parents to the Shroedermans' for a luncheon party.

And so of course Ruby has to help Baker Irving with his flat tire, and the episode ends with Baker Irving making Ruby Redfort French toast, which

is much better than winning a gold medal for
swimming.

It's a typical ending they do in Hollywood,
which never happens in real life.

And so the thing I discover is
    that Ruby never *is* disappointed.
Nothing ever is disappointing for Ruby Redfort.
So you see, for once, she can't help me.

Some things that **Seem** like they are going to be **Dreary** Aren't as dreary as you **Think**

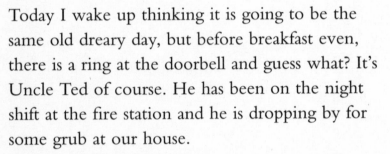

Today I wake up thinking it is going to be the same old dreary day, but before breakfast even, there is a ring at the doorbell and guess what? It's Uncle Ted of course. He has been on the night shift at the fire station and he is dropping by for some grub at our house.

He is always doing this, just turning up when you don't expect it, just out of the blue. It's one of the things I really like about him. He just seems to have the knack of showing up when you need cheering up.

It's a natural talent.

I don't know how he knows.

But he does.

He says, "Hi there, Clarice B. Here's the deal: for a cup of tea and a chocolate cookie, I will drive you to school in my crazy car."

And I say, "You got it," even though it takes about less than 7 minutes to get to school if you are a fast walker, which luckily I am. I just like driving in Uncle Ted's car.

It's the smallest car you've ever seen and it's yellow.

Uncle Ted is almost about seven feet, I think— anyway, tall—and his car is small.

Of course when I go to find the cookies, I remember that I ate them all last night. So I say, "Sorry, Uncle Ted, but I am afraid Minal Cricket ate utterly all of them up—he's a bit greedy when it comes to cookies."

❋ ❋ ❋

When I get to school, I find out it isn't going to be a dreary day there either. We go into our class and there sitting on the desk is Mr. Washington.

He says, "Hi, folks. My name is Mr. Washington. Now, of course, I don't need to tell anybody here what Washington is. You'll all know it's the capital city of the United States."

And before he can say anything else, Grace Grapello goes, "And it's an actual state."

And Betty Moody puts up her hand and says, "Also, Washington is the name of the very first American president."

And Mr. Washington says, "Yes, of course, that's right. So who else has got a name that is also a place or a thing?"

I say, "Well, part of my name is Bean, which is a vegetable, and my last name is Tuesday and that is a day of the week."

And Betty says, "My last name is Moody—but I never am."

My cousin Noah says, "My mom is named Marguerite, which is a flower, and she is from Trinidad and I have been there five times and it's really nice."

And then Mr. Washington and Noah talk about Trinidad and it does sound really nice and I will probably get to go there one time soon because I am related to people from there.

Mr. Washington says his first name is Phil, with a **P**, even though it sounds like it could be an **F**. And it's short for Philip and means "kind to horses."

And Karl Wrenbury says, "My name is Karl and it's *short* for driving Mrs. Wilberton crazy and it *means* being in Mr. Pickering's office quite a lot."

And actually everybody laughs.

Even including Mr. Washington.

❋ ❋ ❋

When we get out of school, Mr. Moody-Call-Me-Cecil is waiting to take Betty to her trumpet lesson. He says, "How was school today?"

And I say, "It was exceptionordinarily undreary because we have a new teacher named Mr. Washington."

And Cecil says, "Exceptionordinarily. What a remarkable word—I might use it myself."

And I say, "Thank you, but Mrs. Wilberton says

I am not supposed to use it because I have made it up and it is not an actual proper word and people can't go around making words up willy-nilly."

And Cecil says, "Nonsense. The dictionary is always growing—that's the wonderful thing. New words are invented every year."

Which reminds me I haven't been learning my spellings for the spelling bee and it is coming up in a few weeks' time and I don't want to stand there like a dodo without a clue.

❋ ❋ ❋

So I say goodbye and nip off home. I find the big dictionary and go up to my room. There are more words in there than I will probably ever use in my whole entire life, even if I live up to 90 or maybe 95.

I don't know where to start.

So I open it on Q because there are less Q words and so I feel less scared of them. In fact one thing that turns out to be quite interesting is that I find out what a **Quahog** is—*a thick-shelled clam of the North Atlantic coast.*

Quandong—*an Australian tree with red fruit that you can make into jam if you want.*

Quip—*a witty remark made on the spur of the moment.* Someone who is good at quips is my dad.

I also find some words that are less useful and I don't really know what they mean even when I read the meaning, i.e., **Quantal**—*relating to a quantum or to a system that has been quantized.*

And there are other words that I just don't think I will use that much.

Quagga—*an extinct stripy mammal from the horse family related to the zebra.*

I am learning the **Q**'s for at least an hour and a quarter and I am realizing that I am quickly taking in a quantity of quite useful vocabulary.

The only thing is I am much more interested in knowing what the words mean than

remembering how to spell them.

Then Dad calls out that it is suppertime and I go downstairs and I say, "I don't mean to quibble, but is it suppertime, dinnertime, or snack time?

Which word is the right word to use? It's just a query—*a request for information.*"

Dad says he will have to think about it.

I say, "Do you ever go to Quebec?"

Dad says, "Quite frequently."

I say, "Do we have any quince juice? As I need to quench my thirst."

Mom says, "No, but we might have some water in the tap."

I say, "Why do we never have quail quiche?"

Mom says, "Because it makes me queasy."

I say, "You sound querulous—*inclined to complain or find fault.*"

She says, "Have you swallowed a dictionary?"

I say, "Am I being a bit of a querist—*someone who asks questions*?"

Minal says, "Mo-om, Clarice is being annoying and she ate a cookie yesterday before supper when you told her not to."

I say, "Quisling"—*which means traitor.*

Mom says, "Quiet"—which means keep it zipped.

❋ ❋ ❋

The next day, we are having some play rehearsals. It is hard for me to concentrate because I don't really have to do much since my scene is really short and I am rather wishing I could go home.

I have still got quite a lot of the Q's to learn and I want to get started on the Y's.

Karl keeps making these faces at me to try and make me laugh. And I can see him out of the corner of my eye trotting up and down doing his Mrs. Wilberton impression.

And I am just in the middle of doing my Robert Granger impersonation back when Mrs. Wilberton goes, "Clarice and Karl, if you find each other so amusing, perhaps you would be amused to spend an hour together in detention. The choice is yours."

Anyway, later in the rehearsal, Karl is having to be Rolf, the boyfriend of Liesl. He is not happy.

Grace is trying to hold his hand because that is part of their dancing routine and every time she lets go, Karl wipes it on his pants.

Mrs. Wilberton says, "Karl, you simply must hold hands with Grace."

Karl says, "Why?"

Mrs. Wilberton says, "Because that's what boyfriends do."

Karl says, "How would you know?"

Luckily Mrs. Wilberton doesn't hear as she is too busy adjusting her piano stool.

Then Mrs. Wilberton says, "Now, Rolf, I want you to *kiss* Liesl on the hand and *twirl* her around."

Karl says, "You must be joking."

Mrs. Wilberton says, "Far from it, young man, now on the double: kiss and twirl."

Karl has a funny look in his eyes and I am surprised to see him not marching off.

Mrs. Wilberton plonks on the piano and Karl grabs Grace's hand and licks it. Grace Grapello screams.

Which I can tell you is very loud and I wouldn't be surprised if I don't have a small amount of deafness in one or two ears now.

Karl says, "There is no way I am going to kiss a girl on the hands, live onstage in front of the whole school."

Mrs. Wilberton is red as a beet. She points at the door and says,

"Mr. Pickering's office, NOW!
We do not
lick other people's hands
in THE SOUND OF MUSIC."

✸ ✸ ✸

When I get home, I go to study some more spellings.

I decide to skip the rest of the Q's and move straight on to the Y's. Don't ask me why.

That night I dream that a youthful yak yearns for some yogurt so it gets aboard a yacht and sails off for years and years but in the end all he finds is a yard full of yellow yams.

Although I can remember what all these words mean, I am still none the wiser on how to spell YACHT.

But it's interesting that reading the dictionary turns out not to be dreary at all, as there are some really good words in there.

That's the thing: some things that are meant to be dreary—are not.

* * *

After Karl did the hand licking, Mr. Pickering said he really couldn't be allowed to play the part of Grace's boyfriend, so now he has the job of sound effects. Which Karl is really pleased about.

We went over to Betty's, and her mom, Mol, gave Karl her tiny tape-recorder machine. He's got all kinds of marvelous noises but I am not sure how he is going to use some of them. Most of them don't really seem like they would be noises that would happen in **THE SOUND OF MUSIC** but Karl Wrenbury is quite clever about these things, so I am sure he will think of something.

Betty's dad, Cecil, says, "How are you getting along with the spelling bee, Clarice?"

I say, "Well, I am trying really hard but although I am studying the dictionary, I am not really remembering any spellings and my spelling is just as bad as it always was."

I say, "The problem is people think you are not so smart if you can't spell."

Cecil says, "But this is not true, because lots of smart people can't spell."

I say, "Like, for example, who?"

Cecil says, "Like, for example, Einstein. ✲ He is a person who most people would say is one of the smartest people ever born."

This of course is true. I have heard of him.

And the reason I have heard of him is because he is famous for being smart. So not being able to spell does not make you unsmart.

I write that in my Ruby notebook.

Einstein—brainy man who couldn't spell.

✲ ✲ ✲

On Friday at our next drama workshop, we do all these special drama exercises and voice thingies and I realize that there is more to acting than just saying your lines and that I can do a lot with my face.

✲ **Einstein**—a man who was very good at sums. What he is famous for is **E=mc²** which is something very clever to do with science.

Czarina says,

*"**Darlinks**, acting is about using your **entire** body and your **whole** self.*

*Use **yourself**, use every inch of you, use yourself up **entirely** — I want to **see** nothing left of you."*

She says,

*"**The very hardest** thing to do in **acting** is to **react**."*

She says this while she is moving about the room in her special shoes and when she says the word

*"**react**"* she suddenly shoots out her arm as if she is going to pinch someone on the nose and everyone ducks.

She says,

*"**You** see, **darlinks**, how you all **reacted** then? Well, can you do it when you **know** what **I** am going to **do**?*

*Isn't it much harder to **act surprised** than **be surprised**?"*

Of course she is completely quite right, and on the way home, me and Betty cannot stop talking about her. She is so amazing.

And I feel all cheerful again, because now when I am playing nun four, I can use my face to show what kind of person nun four is, i.e., not just *a* nun but a nun I have come up with.

And even though I have hardly any lines, I can react to things and make the character interesting.

That's what life is like—sometimes you think everything is dreariness and then you find out it isn't.

It can be
Wrong
to be Right

On Monday I am late for school again because my hair is not doing what it is meant to do and I can't stop it doing what it wants.

I have lost all my hair clips, and the one that I ordered from the back of the Ruby Redfort spaghetti FOUR WEEKS AGO still hasn't arrived. It was a special offer and I had to collect up 6 tokens and send in $1.99 and then they would send you a Ruby Redfort hair clip with a fly on it, just like the one Ruby herself wears and they said I would get my fly clip within 28 days.

one token

But it has not arrived and I am thinking of writing a complaint.

When I do get to school, it turns out to be not such a good day and things go from bad to worserish.

Karl gets banned from the sound effects for doing rude noises whenever Captain von Trapp walks onstage. And I get banned from being nun four because Mrs. Wilberton overheard me saying she has got a big *derrière.*

Which is French for bottom.

She does have a big *derrière.*

This is true, which anyone would agree.

But it seems you are not allowed to say what is true unless you are at least 18 years of age.

And Mrs. Wilberton is in charge of the truth and she gets to say what is allowed to be the truth and what is not. She says, "I think we would *all* appreciate hearing less from you, madam."
Not that she bothers to ask anyone else what they think.

I am now nun seven and have no lines, none.

It's funny how none and nun sound like the same word, because for me being a nun in the school play means no fun, none.

Now I am thinking of not being in **THE SOUND OF MUSIC** at all.

I am fed up with being given the loser parts and told off every five minutes when we are meant to be enjoying ourselves.

During break I go and sit on my own since Betty isn't around. She's at her trumpet lesson.

I have a gnawing worry about the spelling bee, which just won't go away. It seems utterly unfair that someone like Karl is a good speller even though he never even tries and someone like me is a bad speller even though I try quite a lot.

And it's not my fault if I don't know how many **K**'s there are in **anxious**—anxious is a very *anxious-making* word.

Since I have my pocket dictionary with me, I decide to make a start on the **X**'s. What I learn is that nearly no word that sounds like it should begin with an X does begin with an X.

For example, the word example, which begins with an E.

In fact all the X words mainly seem to begin with a zee or zi sound.

This is what you are up against with spelling and it is just the kind of thing that drives me crazy.

X is not a useful beginning to a word, because if it was, then xylophone would not be the only word anyone could think of to put on the alphabet chart. One word that makes sense and is the only word I know with an X that does, is X-RAY, which is what Minal had one time when he fell over and thought he had broken his leg but since he landed on his bottom, they really should have done an x-ray of his bum.

But of course they didn't because they never do.

❊ ❊ ❊

The other thing that made the day a bit worse was that this afternoon Betty got in trouble. This

doesn't usually happen because Betty Moody is one
of those people who simply never gets in trouble
for anything—except after lunch today when Mrs.
Wilberton spelled something on the board and
Betty put her hand up to say she was wrong.

Mrs. Wilberton was trying to write

Sahara Desert

which is a dry place and absolutely everything is
made of sand. You must not go there without at
least 2ish gallons of water or you will simply
shrivel up of drought and probably die.

Although I do have this book about surviving in
absolutely dreadfulish emergencies.

And it is said if you are trapped in a desert with
no water, you must, whatever you do, have an old
baked-bean can with you—empty—although in
an emergency you can always quickly eat the
baked beans. Or if you aren't hungry, pour them
into something else and save them for later.

What you do if you have forgotten your
can opener, I don't know.

Anyway, then what you do is at night put a

plastic bag on top of the can with a small pebble on top, and like magic when you wake up, there will be water in the can.

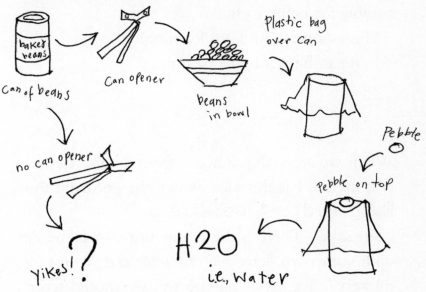

Can of beans

baked beans

Can opener

beans in bowl

Plastic bag over Can

no can opener

Pebble

Pebble on top

Yikes!?

H2O

i.e., Water

I'm not sure how it works, but it's something to do with science.

Anyway, Mrs. Wilberton by accident wrote Sahara Dessert, which is more of an after-dinner treat. Because that's what Desert with two S's means. So she wrote the Sahara Dessert, which does not actually exist. At least I don't think there is a Sahara Dessert.

And if there is, I bet it is really dry.

Mrs. Wilberton did not like being told she was wrong about her spelling. So then Betty was in trouble for being right.

This is something I am learning:

it can be wrong to be right.

✺ ✺ ✺

When we are walking home from school, Betty tells me she has this idea, which she got from the Ruby Redfort website.

She says, "There is this competition to come up with your own detective character and write a mystery." She says, "So you see, we should write our own detective series."

I say, "But I don't think it can be that easy, Betty."

And she says, "Why not?"

And I say, "Because Ruby Redfort is a really clever idea and I could never come up with something as clever as that. It is the most clever book I have ever read, and it is funny."

Betty says, "Think about it: there are all those

books in the stores and even in the supermarkets and if they were that difficult to write, why would there be so many?"

She has a point. That's the thing about Betty Moody: she's a good thinker. If she *is* right about this and we *can* write our own best-selling detective series, then I *really do* need to be able to spell.

Later I am at home doing some spelling practice, trying to work out how many **G**'s there are in jeepers, when there is a ring at the doorbell.

It's Karl. He's come to collect Grandad and Cement for their training. I am going to go along with them because Karl says I can and it's really fun.

Karl is all excited and out of breath and he is waving a piece of paper. It has a number on it.

He says, "Guess what this is?"

And I say, "A piece of paper with a number on it."

And he can't be bothered to laugh at my joke and just carries on talking really speedily.

He says, "Well, guess what? I was looking in my mom's bag because she asked me to get her purse for her, and then this address book fell out and it fell open on the D page, which is what my dad's name begins with—D—Damon. And I didn't look on purpose or anything, but it was just lying there open and it was my dad's number so I scribbled it down before she could know that I had seen it and she doesn't know and you can't tell anyone, ever—I mean it."

I say, "I won't—I promise—but I thought your mom said she didn't have your dad's number. I thought no one knew where your dad had gone."

Karl says, "I don't know why she did that. Anyway, I am going to call him maybe this weekend and I am going to ask him if I can come and live with him, wherever that is."

I say, "Wow, are you? That's really exciting."

Karl says, "I know."

And I say, "I wonder why your mom didn't tell you she had your dad's number when she did."

And he says, "I don't know. Anyway, it's going to be really good living with him."

And I say, "But what if he says no? What will you do then?"

He says, "He's not GOING to say NO."

I say, "I am not saying he is. I only meant what will you do if he does?"

And he says, "Look, I am trying to tell you something good. I have found my dad's number and I am GOING to go and live with him."

I say, "I know, I know—it is really good and it's utterly good you have found your dad's number but I was only wondering why your mom didn't tell you."

Karl says, "You don't even KNOW my DAD. Of COURSE my DAD wants me to live with him. Why wouldn't he?"

I say, "I wasn't saying he wouldn't, just what if he didn't?"

Karl says,

"Why do you have to be like that? I KNEW I shouldn't have bothered talking to YOU—you are just like EVERYONE ELSE." Then he runs off.

I feel bad because I was only trying to say the right thing but maybe I am saying the wrong thing. I am not sure anymore.

But it's strange that Karl's mom wouldn't tell Karl about his dad's number when she knew it all the time—so you see I can't help thinking she has a reason.

Maybe it's like that thing Ruby said:

"Sometimes it's better for people not to be in the know—if what they know ain't good to know."

So you see, I was only saying something that Ruby herself would say.

And Ruby is usually right.

So why do I feel so bad?

Sometimes you do not Expect to feel Better but then, you just Do

9

It is an amazing thing how the human-being person recovers from disappointment and dreadful happenings. And this is because of the human brain, and due to it being a mysterious thing.

I heard a man on television say that **the human brain is more complicated than an actual computer**. Which I doubt sometimes.

And so would you if you had met Robert Granger. The man said,

"The brain is an incredible, ingenious thing."

And this is true. It is **incomprehensible**—*very difficult to understand*—almost, how it can feel sad one minute and hopeful the next.

And how does it think of all kinds of things at once?

The memory is the strangest thing of all and I am not sure how it works.

Sometimes it is utterly a blank.

And *why* it chooses to remember things like we had sausages last Thursday but it cannot remember the eight times table is a mystery.

My memory would rather remind me about how Mrs. Wilberton had spinach stuck on her tooth and how I tripped over in front of my whole class last week and some people probably got to see my underwear, which to be actually honest, I would rather forget.

At drama workshop, Czarina says,

"All the stuff you think of as 'useless information' can be quite useful for your acting."

And that

"Darlink, tripping over in front of everybody could turn out to be quite a good thing in the end."

She says,

"You must use those experiences.
They are food for acting; they nourish
your craft. Write them down."

I say, "The last thing I want to do is tell any more people how I tripped over and people saw my underwear."

The worst bit is, they were absolutely embarrassing ones and they had a picture of a little monkey on them and that is not me— I do not wear stupid underwear normally. Which is why Granny would say every day should be best-underwear day to avoid this kind of a disaster.

Anyway, Czarina says,

"These kind of memories are useful
because the secret to fabulous acting is
understanding how something like, for example,
falling over in front of your whole class and being
completely embarrassed, might feel.
Darlink, the more experiences you have like
this, the better you will become at imagining,
inventing, and embodying."

On the way home, I am wondering if nun seven

was ever embarrassed in front of her whole class. And I am wondering whether she decided to become a nun because one day she fell over and everyone got to see her monkey pants. And I make a note of this in my Ruby Redfort notebook.

And I am thinking, I am really getting to know nun seven. She's a bit like nun four but not quite exactly the same because I have made her different and I think I will be good at acting her.

﹡ ﹡ ﹡

The next time we have Mr. Washington, I ask him about the memory thing because I desperately want to remember all my spellings and also other things too. Things that might come in useful. Like for example, there are things you think you don't need to remember, things that you don't think would be helpful but then suddenly you find out they are.

Like knowing nine eights are whatever nine eights ﹡ are.

﹡ $9 \times 8 = 72$

Or how far it is to walk from Helsinki to Constantinople ❀ because you never know when you might have to.

Then there are other things that are nice to remember because they are nice to remember—like for example maybe a poem.

Or the name of a mountain in Japan,

just because it's nice to know.

My dad's one of those people who is always remembering things. You can ask him practically anything about facts and he will know the answer.

He says if he doesn't know the answer, then he will just come up with one because why not?

He says, "Just give it a try."

A Ruby Redfort rule is YOU JUST NEVER KNOW WHEN SOMETHING YOU KNOW IS GONNA COME IN HANDY.

So this is a good reason to know more. But the thing is, however much I know, I always forget it.

Mr. Washington says, "The secret is to train your memory." He says, "It's just like exercising

❀ **Constantinople** (now called Istanbul) is 1,332 miles from Helsinki. 1 mile will take 20-ish minutes if you are a fastish walker. So it will take you 26,640 minutes to get there. But don't forget to stop for a fizzy drink or you will die of drought.

any other part of your body. There are things you can do to get it in shape."

He says, "The first thing to do is try and memorize something you really enjoy. Like maybe a poem or a song or breeds of dogs or whatever you are really into."

He says, "The secret is to be interested. Is there something you would really like to be able to say by heart?"

And I say, "Well, it's funny, because I nearly know the whole part of Liesl in **THE SOUND OF MUSIC**—I have sort of learned it by accident, just listening to Grace doing it over and over."

And Mr. Washington says, "Well, that's probably because you would love to play this part so your mind is interested. So why don't you learn the whole part perfectly? It will be really good practice."

I think he is right and I should start to train my memory.

Then I think of Karl training Grandad and Cement and I wonder if it will be so easy.

❋ ❋ ❋

On Saturday there is nothing to do and so I slightly wander along to Eggplant. It is very hot and there is nobody out on our street at all except for a few flies. When I turn the corner onto Sesame Park Road, there are people everywhere and I can see them all plonked out like sardines in the park.

Eggplant is all nice and cool, and for once there is no one in there except for Kurt and this other girl who works there. Kurt seems really pleased to see me and he even introduces me to the girl, who is named Kira.

She has her hair done in a scarf and wears very wide-legged pants that are all fraying at the ends and she has got an earring in her eyebrow.

It looks very uncomfortable and she keeps twiddling it.

She and Kurt are in the kind of mood where everything each other says is funny. And they keep chasing each other around the shop trying to stick price labels onto the other one's pants.

When they have stopped doing this, Kurt says, "What's going on in our street?"

And I say, "Just a few flies buzzing around."

And Kira finds this very funny and says, "Wow, your sister is funny, man."

I think she is from New York.

And she gives me a juice that is not a juice really, more like yellow water, and it tastes slightly of the shop.

Kira says, "It's got lots of Chinese herbs in it and is good if you are detoxing." ✳

I say, "I am not sure if I am detoxing" because I don't know what detoxing is but I drink it anyway, even though it is the color of pee.

I make a note in my Ruby notebook to

✳ **Detoxing**—treatment to help your body get rid of nasty bits and bobs that it would be better off without.

look up the word detoxing in my dictionary when I get home.

We are all having a very nice time chatting and I am allowed to sit on the shop assistant's stool, which I have always wanted to do because it is very high, and they give me one of the Eggplant T-shirts to wear so I actually sort of look like I am a short person who works in the shop.

Then suddenly all these girls come in. They are all talking very fast and quite loudly and they all giggle at the same time. And they ask if they can have freshly squeezed juices from the juice bar. But they don't ask Kira. They ask Kurt and he goes a bit distracted.

And Kira seems really fed up and I give her this look where one of your eyebrows goes up and she does it back.

I get myself a pure fruit, nothing-added Popsicle from the freezer and leave the money on the counter.

And I say, "Bye, Kira. Bye, Kurt."
But he doesn't hear.
Kira says, "See you around, kid."

Which is exactly the kind of thing Ruby Redfort would say.

I meander along the street sucking my Popsicle, which is the flavor of a mango. I love mango. I love it so much I don't think I will ever go off it.

Then who do I see but Karl Wrenbury. I shout out, "Hi, Karl." But he doesn't hear me so I shout again and wave and I cannot believe he doesn't hear that, so I run after him and grab him on the arm and he says,

"Leave me ALONE, would you"

and he is still walking and I say,

"Karl, it's me, Clarice Bean."

He says, "So?" and I am amazed that he would be like that and I say, "I thought we were friends" and he says, "Yeah? Well, you thought WRONG."

And I just stand there like a fish with my mouth open.

And I watch him walk off and then I trip on the pavement and drop my Popsicle and my toe is bleeding because I am wearing flip-flops and Mom says, "Never ever run in flip-flops" and she is right.

It hurts but I hardly feel it because I am so completely astounded. And I watch my Popsicle melting into the pavement and it doesn't take long and all these ants appear from nowhere and start using the juice like a paddling pool.

And I don't look up because I don't want to start crying so I just stare and stare at the ants swimming in the Popsicle juice and they look like they are having fun.

Then all of a sudden I am picked up off my feet and I am flung in the air and I know who it is of course because he never just says hello or anything normal. The only person he doesn't pick up and fling in the air is my dad because he wouldn't like it and Grandad because he is too fragile and he might break a hip.

And I say, "Uncle Ted, put me down!"

But I don't mean it and we both know it.

And Uncle Ted says, "It's not the sort of day for standing looking at ants, you know."

And I say, "I know that."

And he says, "Well, good, let's go to the movies then."

So we do go to the movies and we have a really
good time and it's nice and cool in there and
nearly empty.

And the movie is about a lost fish whose dad is
trying to find him and it's quite good even though
you do know what's going to happen in the end.
It makes me think of Karl though because it is a
strange thing that his dad is not coming to look
for him.

But however worried I am feeling about Karl
Wrenbury and him saying we are not friends
anymore, it all goes away slightly when I am with
Uncle Ted.

You see, if Uncle Ted can't make you laugh, no
one can. But after he has gone and I am home, I
start to think about Karl again and what he said
and it makes me feel sick inside and when Dad
says "suppertime,"

I am not hungry.

Sometimes there are Things you would Rather Not Know

The next day I watch TV.

Clancy Crew and Ruby Redfort are hiding out after school. They are watching out for suspicious behavior and strange goings-on. Which of course there is a lot of in Twinford.

RUBY: "Hey, Clance, would ya take a look at this—"

Ruby passes her special sunglasses, which are actually a pair of binoculars in disguise, to Clancy and he puts them on.

CLANCY: "Well, whadda ya know—isn't that Barney Herbert, the super-geek talking to Bugwart?"

RUBY: "You better believe it, buster. Boy, the stuff you see when you are hanging out on surveillance! You can learn a lot about folks if you just sit back and watch."

CLANCY: "You got that right. I wouldn't have believed it if I hadn't seen it with my own two eyes."
RUBY: "Since when did Vapona Bugwart start getting friendly with geeks? She's gotta be up to something."
CLANCY: "Howdaya know?"
RUBY: "Because she always is. I'll bet you she probably wants to use his computer or borrow his new bike. She wouldn't suck up to him for no reason—you can be sure of that."

Just then, while Clancy and Ruby are being all distracted, a sinister-looking black car drives up—they don't see it because they are too busy being distracted and that is something that undercover secret agents must never be.

Do you see what's happened?

Ruby Redfort has broken one of her own golden Ruby Redfort rules: NEVER GET DISTRACTED BY THE LITTLE THINGS WHEN SOMETHING BIG IS GOING DOWN.

And this just goes to prove that even someone like Ruby Redfort who is a brilliant genius can slip up from time to time and forget the most important of things.

❀ ❀ ❀

I decide to do some surveillance of my own, i.e., watch to see if someone is up to anything. So I get my Ruby notebook and go and sit outside my house in a chair so I can accidentally see what interesting things are going on in our street.

It is a very hot day and after 22 minutes I am parched to a crisp and only a meager cat with a limp has walked by. It would be all right if I was sitting here with Clancy Crew. He is a great sort of friend to have, and I start thinking about Karl Wrenbury and how I wish he would come and sit in a chair with me but he is not talking to me anymore. So that's that, really.

Cat with a limp

Mrs. Stampney comes out and flaps a tea towel and says, "Does your mother know you are sitting out front doing nothing?"

I say, "I am not doing nothing. I am watching things."

She says, "Being a nosy parker more like."

I say, "Takes one to know one."

I say that under my breath because the last thing I want is Mrs. Stampney on my tail. Especially when I am on surveillance.

Hitch always says, "Ruby, don't attract the attention of members of the public—they will blow your cover." Ruby is a bit hotheaded and often gets into trouble because she can't stop herself from telling people what's what.

Ruby and me have this in common slightly.

Mrs. Stampney goes back indoors and pretends she isn't looking at me through her lace curtains. And I pretend that I am not noticing that she is looking at me through her lace curtains.

That's a Ruby Redfort rule: NEVER LET THE ENEMY KNOW THAT YOU KNOW THAT THEY KNOW.

Pretending not to know things is much harder work than you might think.

I can hear Robert Granger's loud voice. He lives next door, and he is playing in his paddling pool—and I wouldn't be surprised if he doesn't pop it, the way he is bouncing about.

As much as I don't want to talk to Robert Granger, I do really want a go in his paddling pool because I am really hot as a lobster and will probably overheat at any moment and start gibbering—the heat can make you do that if you are not careful.

And it can be known for people to go into utter madness of the brain.

I decide to take emergency action to avoid this possibility. I go into the yard and call over the wall. I say, "Hello, Robert Granger. Is that a paddling pool?"

And he says, "No, it's a plunge pool ✳ in actual fact." Which it is not, but I don't say anything because I want to go in it.

So instead I say, "Oh, it looks really good. I've never been in a plunge pool before."

And he says, "Do you want to try it?"

Which of course I do since otherwise I would not be talking to him. I say really casually, "OK, why not? Just for a minute or two."

✳ **Plunge pool**—a special mini pool for cooling down in, often found in Hollywood, i.e., not a little, titchy pool found in Robert Granger's yard.

I am already in my bathing suit for speed and I climb over the back wall and nip into the pool. It's worth it for 5 minutes but as soon as I have cooled down, I begin to see the error of my ways. Plus he may have peed in it.

Luckily for me, Mom calls, "Clarice, Betty's on the phone."

I say, "Sorry, Robert, but I will have to take that call."

And he shouts, "Come right back, won't you."

And I feel a teensy bit bad because I know I will not go right back—I will nip over to Betty's as soon as I possibly can.

Betty is all very excited because she has been to the updated Ruby Redfort website. It has loads of new facts about the author, Patricia F. Maplin Stacey, although I notice they still have the picture of her looking very youngish when I happen to know she is more like 72 or so.

They also have printed on the website Ruby Redfort Code, * just like she uses in the

---

※ **Ruby Redfort Code,** e.g., **bad** = **tapioca**, because tapioca is a horrible pudding; **good** = **pizza**, because pizza is delicious; **trouble** = **dirty dog**, because dirty dogs don't smell good.

books—so you can learn how to speak it.

It sounds really complicated at first and you don't think it would be possible to ever get the hang of it, but then you get to know how it works and you see how it's done—and you realize that she has just swapped the meanings of the words around. It's a bit like a whole new language, and me and Betty are going to learn it so we can speak secretly to each other without anyone else being able to understand.

When you click on the website, the voice of Hitch comes on and goes, "Glad you could make it, kid," which is something he always says in the books. He is the new Hitch, the Hollywood one, and he is named George Conway.

Betty says, "Look, it even has a picture of the new Ruby Redfort who will be in the movie."

She looks a bit like me but with less tangly hair and more oomph. She is named Skyler Summer. I say, "I wish I was named Skyler Summer. I have such an unstarry name. Someone who is called Skyler Summer is much more likely to be in a Hollywood movie than someone called Clarice Bean Tuesday."

Betty says, "I think Clarice Bean Tuesday is a very good name to have and it sounds utterly like a writer or an organic muffin."

Maybe she is right and it is not so bad for a name.

Names are interesting things because they are just words but they can make you feel differently about someone.

It's a bit like what Mr. Washington was talking about—how they all sort of mean things and how the sound of your name can be important.

If you don't know someone but you like their name, you sort of expect to like them, at least at first.

And if they have a pretty name, you sort of expect them to be pretty.

And if they have a cool sort of name like Clancy Crew, you expect them to be coolish.

And if someone has a rarish name you are much more likely to remember them.

Names are very important. I mean, when you hear the name Hogtrotter, you just know he is not going to be a pleasant type.

Mr. Washington's name makes me want to go to

Washington because I like him and it makes me wonder if I would like Washington the place.

My name is sort of unusual so people tend to remember me.

Which can be good and can be bad.

Depending.

✸ ✸ ✸

I am mooching back from Betty's trying to think of a name I would like to be called more than Clarice Bean and I am suddenly distracted by shouting coming out of the telephone booth on Sesame Park Road. And just as I am about to walk past, the door flings open and Karl Wrenbury comes running out.

And for one single second he turns around and he sees me and I see him and I know that it looks like he might be nearly in tears.

And I know he will hate me for seeing this and he runs off so fast I can't even say anything even if I could have thought of anything to say.

I look down at the ground and there are

0

2 9 7

4 4

5

lots of tiny pieces of paper like a tiny trail.

I collect them all up
and I put them all together
and all the tiny pieces of paper make a number
and underneath the number
there is a smiley face drawn.
And I know what it is.
It is Karl's dad's phone
number.

86

9

Sometimes there are Things that people will Never know You Know

On Monday Karl Wrenbury won't even look at me, let alone say hello.

It is making me quite down in the dumps so I am very pleased we are having a Mr. Washington class.

Mr. Washington has asked everyone to do a picture of the inside of their head. He doesn't mean the actual inside of your head, how it would look with all the brains and wriggly bits and everything. He means all the whirling thoughts and information and how does it feel sometimes when you are fed up or in a rage or chirpy or utterly bored.

Draw that.

It's a really good thing to draw because there's no wrong or right. Mr. Washington says there hardly ever is an utterly wrong or utterly right, especially when it comes to saying what is going on inside your own head.

He says, "Sometimes a mistake is what shows you how to do something, so how can you say your mistake was wrong?"

Of course he is right.

How can a mistake be a mistake?

By mistake, when I was making fudge one time, I over-bubbled it and got it too hot and when I tried to eat it, it had turned into toffee. And I wouldn't have known this could happen if I hadn't made a mistake with the bubbling.

We are learning things all the time.

That's what Mr. Washington says.

I know what he means—I am nonstop learning. I am learning things just walking down the street and also I am learning things when I am asleep because things float in and out of my head.

I'm even learning things when I am reading Ruby Redfort under the desk in Mrs. Wilberton's class.

Mr. Washington says, "It's good to be able to read and write; it helps us to communicate. And where would we be without numbers? You can't always rely on a calculator to do your numbers."

It's true, because you wouldn't know what age you were without numbers, and you do need to be able to add things up in your head, because what if your calculator broke?

Mr. Washington says, "But there are other things just as important, and many of these we learn by accident."

I have found out a lot of new things by accident and I am learning all the time.

One thing I have learned in Mr. Washington's class is that the stars are always there but we only see them in the dark.

One thing I have discovered by accident is that you can get sunburned even on a cloudy day.

I say to Mr. Washington, "But Mr. Washington, I definitely want to be able to communicate, but spelling doesn't always help. There are words like spell and spell and they look the same but they don't mean the same but how would you know? I mean it's confusing. One means something to do with *magic* and one means having to put *letters* in the right order.

"Then there's words like bear and bare. One sort of bear is an *animal covered in fur,* and the other sort of bare means *being covered in nothing,* and they *sound* the same but they are *spelled* differently and what's the point of that? Words shouldn't sound the same if they aren't spelled the same."

Mr. Washington says, "CB, that's a very good point. I know it can be very complicated and it's not easy, but maybe the thing is to think of spelling like some sort of code with lots of secret rules—the trick is to crack it and find ways of *remembering* the rules.

"Take the word PIECE—as in 'How about a PIECE of PIE?' All you have to do is remember that PIE is in the word PIECE.

"And then how about HEAR, as in listening—it is just EAR with an H at the front. And if you remember that you need to use your EAR to HEAR, you will never forget how to spell that kind of HEAR.

"And what about NECESSARY? Karl, I see you've got a shirt on and it's got ONE collar—

that's ONE C, and TWO sleeves—that's TWO
S's, and so if you think about your shirt, you will
always know how to spell NECESSARY."

This is very useful information, so I write it into
my Ruby notebook and draw a picture of a pie,
an ear, a collar, and two sleeves.

Thinking of spelling as a code makes me think of
Ruby. She knows loads of codes. I wonder how
she ever learned them all.

I am only trying to learn one. Which is English.
And I am finding it utterly tricky.

If I was the one who invented spelling,
    I would have done a much better job.
    For instance, why isn't SEA spelled **C**?

On Tuesday Mr. Washington is trying to help us with the spelling bee and he writes up this sentence on the board.

It says,

ATE RUBARB-EATING
RINOCEROSES DANCED WHILE
XITEDLY RECITING RYMES.

Then he says, "Some of these words are spelled correctly and some are not—some of them have silent letters in them and some of them don't. Can anyone come and correct the spelling in this sentence for me?"

Lots of people put up their hands, but Mr. Washington picks Karl Wrenbury. I am surprised that Karl wants to do this, he normally is not one for putting up his hand, even if he does know the answer.

But he is really good at spelling and he makes the sentence look like this.

EIGHT rHubARB-EATING
RINOCEROSES DANCED WHILE
ExCITEDLY RECITING rHymES.

Mr. Washington says, "Nice work, Karl. In fact very nearly perfect—you only missed one. Can anyone spot the other mistake?"

I put my hand up to tell Mr. Washington that I know about **rhinoceros**. I know it has a secret **H** in it.

It's one word I know because of staring at my rhinoceros poster every night. And even though Karl is a really good speller, I know about the **H** and he doesn't. And I am a bit worried to say it, now that Karl doesn't like me anymore, but I really want people to know that **rhinoceros** is a word I can spell.

Mr. Washington finally spots me and says, "Yes, **CB**, can you tell us what word Karl has missed?"

And I am just about to say the answer when Mr. Skippard, the janitor, pops his head around the door and says, "I would just like everyone to know that starting tomorrow, the back playground will not be in use because we will have builders in, mending the roof. Therefore, it is out of bounds. Please make sure you do not leave any bikes in the bike shed because

you will not be able to get them for several
weeks."

Then he goes.

And then the bell rings.

And then everyone goes.

And I am not able to say my one thing that I
know about spelling.

Sometimes you've just got to **Sit Tight** and See what **Happens**

Mrs. Wilberton gives us some homework called "My Weekend." She wants us to write about what happened over the weekend, i.e., this last one just gone.

Karl says he won't do it. Mrs. Wilberton asks, "Why not?"

And I remember him on Sunday in the phone booth and I know this is not something Karl would want to write about.

Karl says, "Because it's my own private business and nobody is going to know my stuff."

Mrs. Wilberton says, "Don't be so ridiculous. You will do the writing just like everybody else."

Karl says, "You CAN'T make me."

Mrs. Wilberton says, "We'll see about that, Karl Wrenbury."

The bell rings and Karl storms out of the room and Mrs. Wilberton shouts after him, "I will be calling your mother."

And Karl shouts back, "GOOD LUCK."

Mrs. Wilberton shouts,

"Karl Wrenbury, you had better turn up with your homework tomorrow or you will be in very big trouble, young man . . .

I MEAN IT."

And Karl turns around and I see his face.

And I do not think I would like to be in Mrs. Wilberton's shoes.

✻ ✻ ✻

I am going over to Betty's house after school. We are both quite wondering what Karl will do next because we can't help feeling he will definitely do something. I am not sure if I should do something myself. You know, to stop him.

Before he goes too far.

But he is not listening to me anymore.

When me and Betty get to her house, we run up to the kitchen to make some sandwiches and switch on the TV because Ruby Redfort is on.

We are watching for detective research as well as because we are mad about it.

The thing I love about the Ruby Redfort TV series is that it is always exciting and quite impossible how to imagine Ruby will get out of the death-defying situation she is in and mostly I spend the whole time behind a chair or grabbing a cushion and the strange thing is that however scary or disastrous things get, Hitch is always so calm and his hair is actually always brushed.

Ruby just about always loses her glasses and Hitch somehow always finds them.

In this episode, which is called,

CAN YOU HEAR ME, CLANCY CREW?

Clancy Crew is bicycling along this road because he has had a message from Ruby that says, "Meet me at the old barn."

But the message isn't from Ruby at all— Clancy

just thinks it is. In fact it is from the evil villain Count von Viscount. And Ruby is on the radio controls because she needs to warn him about a dreadful plan that Count von Viscount has got up his sleeve.

Ruby is on the walkie-talkie saying, "Clance, do you read me? You are in danger. Turn back. Don't go too far. Over."

And Clancy doesn't reply because his walkie-talkie has been blocked by Hogtrotter and Ruby is getting more desperate and going, "Clancy, can you hear me? Can you hear me, Clancy?" And it is beginning to dawn on Clancy as he walks into the barn that something is up and that he has lost walkie-talkie contact and he looks toward the door and says, "Where are you, Ruby? Where to goodness are you?"

Ruby says to Hitch, "He's not listening to me. I just can't get through to him. Why would he turn his walkie-talkie off? He should know that, Hitch—it's one of the rules: NEVER TURN YOUR WALKIE-TALKIE OFF."

Hitch looks worried and one of his eyebrows does this dipping thing—that's how you know when Hitch is worried—and he says, "What if he didn't turn his walkie-talkie off? What if someone else did?"

And then Hitch looks at Ruby and Ruby looks at Hitch, and Ruby looks out of the TV screen and says, "Keep your cool, Clance, my old friend. Don't do anything stupid."

And Clancy is standing alone in the barn or at least we think he is alone until we see a shadow of a hand and Clancy says to himself, "Oh, Rube, if only you were here—you'd know what to do."

And then Hitch looks out of the TV and says, "Sit tight—kid, we're gonna get you out of there."

You don't know what Ruby is going to do but you know she's going to do something.

And you just know that's exactly when the episode's going to end because you are all just completely dying to know what happens next.

After the show Betty Moody is talking about the detective story she wants us to write.

I am still not so sure I can, but Betty asks her mom, Mol, what she thinks.

Mol writes books for a living.

Betty says, "Mol, do you think me and Clarice could write a book?"

And Mol says, "Yes, anyone can write a book. It's writing a good book—that's the trick."

Betty says, "Do you think we could write a good book?"

And Mol says, "As long as you have something to say and an interesting way of saying it."

Betty says, "So that's yes! We have lots of things to say, lots, and Clarice Bean and me always find ourselves interesting, so I am sure other people will too."

❋ ❋ ❋

On my way home, I think about what Mol said about writing. Because it's true—I *do* have things to say, even if nothing exciting *does* happen in my life.

And I think my spelling might be getting better now that I have been doing all this dictionary learning. Which I have been doing a lot of— mainly because I do not want to be absolutely embarrassed in front of the whole school during the spelling bee.

Ruby Redfort always says, "If you put your mind to it, you can do anything." That's what I like about Ruby: she has a go at anything at all. She's not scared of trying and she's brainy and she's a good runner and she still looks like a girl and everything and is utterly pretty but she is also the funny one—not like those girls who go into Eggplant and think Kurt is so hilarious.

If Ruby Redfort went into Eggplant, Kurt would be laughing at Ruby's jokes, I bet you.

And I am walking back home and I have to go past the school and I am quite utterly engrossed and completely absorbed in what I am thinking when I hear a very bewildering noise.

A bit like a snake or the sound of hairspray.

It's coming from the other side of the school wall. Someone must be in the back playground, but why?

And what are they doing?

And how did they get there?

I will write this information down later because there isn't time to unlock my notebook again and I don't want to miss the action.

I really want to know what it is, so I climb up, wedging my foot on a bit of the bricks that are sticking out slightly, and I manage to grab the top of the wall and try to hoist myself up so I can see over but then my foot slips and I scrape my knee and I panic and let go of my notebook and it falls on the other side.

And then what I hear is nothing and then something clatters on the ground like a tin can or something tinny or cannish.

And then what I hear is fastish running. So it was definitely not a snake.

I look down at my knee and it is almost severed off and really bleeding and I will have to hobble home because I don't have a walkie-talkie to radio for help and there is no Hitch to pick me up in the limousine.

And now I will never know who it was
    or what they were doing.

Unless I can find some clues tomorrow.

But I can't write that down because I no longer have my notebook.

Sometimes when you Need things to get Better, they just get Worse

Of course the next day I rush into school because I want to rescue my notebook before anyone finds it. Even though I have the key safe and sound around my neck, I don't want to risk anyone stealing it, because you see, it is the kind of thing that everybody would want. So it is tempting.

The problem is, when I try to get around to the back playground, there is all this fencing stuff up and that's when I remember Mr. Skippard's words. He said this would happen and that the builders would come.

So I have no choice. I will just have to wait and maybe I will never see my Ruby notebook ever again. Who knows? . . .

After lunch, things go even more wrong and something really bad happens.

It all starts with Mrs. Wilberton saying, "I hope everyone has remembered to bring in their homework—'My Weekend'—because we are going to go around the class reading them all out loud."

When she is saying this, she all the time has her beady eyes on Karl Wrenbury. Karl is just sitting there with his arms folded, not even opening his bag.

When Mrs. Wilberton gets to him, she says, "Chop chop, Karl, let's get on with it."

Karl says, "No."

Mrs. Wilberton says, "What do you think makes you so special?"

He says, "Nothing."

Mrs. Wilberton says, "Well then, we will start with you."

Karl says, "Well, I am not going to read anything because I didn't do it."

Mrs. Wilberton says, "I sincerely hope I am hearing wrong because I seem to remember asking you in no uncertain terms to get it done."

Karl says, "You can't make me write about my private stuff and I am not going to."

Mrs. Wilberton says, "You will do what I tell you to do, young man."

Then Karl says,

"I am NOT talking about my private business to you so STOP being such a nosy parker. I hate YOU and I HATE this school."

Then Karl goes completely demented and crazy and chucks all the things off his desk and he throws his chair across the room and he is screaming and screaming.

And our class is all quiet and Mrs. Wilberton goes very pale in the face and a bit shaky and she says, "Now, stop that at once, Karl," but she doesn't say it very loud because she looks sort of shocked.

And Karl is pulling his own hair and he just says over and over, "No one gets to know about my private stuff, no one. I decide who knows my stuff. It's my business, not yours."

And Mrs. Wilberton is panicking and rushes out of the class and comes back in one minute with Mr. Washington, and Mr. Washington walks in all calmly and he says, "Karl, hey, why don't we go outside?" and he just stops all the shouting, just like that.

And Karl looks at him and nods and Mr. Washington says to Mrs. Wilberton, "I'll take it from here."

And Mrs. Wilberton just nods. Because maybe she doesn't know what to say.

And when they go out, no one says a word.

A bit later Mr. Pickering comes in and says, "Does anyone know what brought this on?"

I don't say anything because I am trying to keep my mouth shut and although I know what has upset Karl Wrenbury, he told me not to tell, so I don't.

But I sort of wish I had.

Because how can anyone help if nobody tells?

Some things are True
but not
Completely
True

14

Karl Wrenbury has been given his last and final warning from Mr. Pickering.

And there will be no more chances.

Even though Mr. Washington tried his best.

I know this because I overheard Mrs. Marse talking to Mrs. Wilberton.

This means that one more slip-up and Karl has to leave our school. This makes me sad, because even though Karl has decided not to be my friend anymore, I think school will not be the same without him.

✳ ✳ ✳

When I get home, I rush in and turn on the TV. I am sitting there watching Ruby Redfort.

It's before dinner and I am quite **ravenous**— *really hungry*. And my tummy is making those kind of burbling sounds which if I was hiding in a hedge spying on someone would really give me away. Which is why Ruby always carries a special Ruby cookie in her backpack. They are "highly nutritious and fend off hunger"—that's what they say on the ads. They sell them at our supermarket.

Mom rarely lets me have them because she says they are commercial rubbish and really one is just paying for the packaging. I love the packaging— that's what I like about them. I will buy nearly anything with Ruby Redfort on it.

In this episode, called

HANG IN THERE, BUDDY,

Ruby has got herself in a very tight spot trying to rescue Clancy Crew. Count von Viscount has set the dogs on her and what's worse is, her special bike with rocket boosters has got a flat so she has to ditch it and run like a mad crazy thing to get away.

And Ruby Redfort might be the fastest runner in her school, but can she run faster than a dog?

The answer is no because no one can, I don't think—unless it is a sausage dog. *

Sausage + dog = Sausage dog

And it's no use hiding from dogs because you know what dogs are like . . .

Good smellers, and they will find you wherever, even if you are running

in a stream of water—they will sniff you out.

If you want to outwit a dog, Karl Wrenbury says you must confuse them with different odors so they don't know what they are chasing anymore. Easier said than done.

Luckily Ruby knows this and has brought some of her really smelly socks, which she puts on a

* **Sausage dog** (Proper name: dachshund). Looks like a sausage on legs. Good at smelling things out but doesn't have a personal scent like other dogs.

passing deer, who runs off in them. Which of course the dogs follow thinking it is Ruby herself.

And then she sprays this special deodorizing spray all over herself, which dissolves all her odor and gives her the smell of a shrub so she can simply blend in.

You can see what I mean about amazing ideas. It just wouldn't occur to me to do that.

Then she says, "Sniff that, suckers!"

I love watching Ruby Redfort because it just sort of carries me away. I almost feel like I am her.

And I find myself saying things like "Oh, brother" and "This is a total yawn." She has an amazing way of talking. I am trying to perfect it myself.

And the other day when I got home from being at Betty's, I walked in and my dad was reading the paper in his glasses and Mom was doing some knitting and Minal was making something out of toilet-paper rolls and I said, "What is this, geek central?"

And Dad looked up from his reading and dipped his eyebrow and said, "Glad you could make it, KID."

And I said, "I didn't know you knew Hitch's catch phrase."

And he said, "Well, KID, you learn something NEW every day." Which is exactly what Hitch would say.

And I said, "You got that right." Which is exactly what Clancy Crew would say.

And Mom said, "You better believe it, buster." Which is exactly what Ruby Redfort would say.

And Minal said, "What are you talking about?"

Which is exactly what I would expect from my maggot brother.

Anyway, I am sitting watching Ruby Redfort but in the ad breaks I am keeping half an ear out for intriguing information. Sometimes you can pick up top-secret things when you are watching TV since nobody thinks you are listening.

I hear Grandad talking to Cement, our dog. He says, "How would you like a nice bit of steak? Oh, I bet you would like that, wouldn't you? Yes, you would—I'll just cut a little bit off each one and no one will ever know. I won't tell if you won't."

Then I hear a gulping sound of a largish dog and a shuffling sound of someone who wears slippers.

I go back to watching the ads. They have one for Ruby spaghetti—it's bits of spaghetti all made into words that Ruby Redfort would say. Things like "creep" and "yeeks" and "bozo."

You see, sometimes Ruby's butler Hitch will write top-secret information in the spaghetti. Her parents are completely **oblivious about**—*unaware of, paying no attention to*—Ruby's secret-agent life.

At dinner Mom says, "I haven't seen Karl around much lately. How's he getting on these days?"

I say, "He has been in more trouble and Mr. Pickering says he will have to think about asking Karl to leave the school and go to another one because he has done all he can and if Karl wants to carry on with this sort of behavior without explaining himself, then he really has no choice but to write to his mother and ask her to find an alternative school for him and he would

regret to do this but he must think long and hard
about the other pupils and what's best for them
and it's a shame, it really is—that's what I heard
Mrs. Marse saying to Mrs. Wilberton that Mr.
Pickering had said to Karl anyway."

Mom says, "Wow, you certainly do pay attention
when you want to."

I say, "Well, that's because this is the kind of
information that interests me."

Mom says, "And what do you think should
happen?"

And I say, "Well, it is difficult for Mr. Pickering
because Karl won't talk to anyone and so no one
knows his problems."

Mom says, "What are his problems?"

And I say, "Karl doesn't want me to say."

And Mom says, "I see the problem."

When Mom serves up the steaks, she says,
"That's funny—they seem much smaller than
when I bought them."

I notice Grandad is looking all age-ed and not
like a person who fed our dinner to the dog. I
don't tell on him because I don't like people who

tell on people and he would be in serious trouble and I like Grandad even if my steak did end up the size of a peanut.

It's a Ruby Redfort rule that SOMEONE'S BAD LUCK COULD BE YOUR GOOD LUCK. And I think she might just be right.

This morning I got to school and I did some overhearing. Which I wished I could have jotted down in my Ruby notebook.

What I heard was Suzie Woo saying to Bridget Garnett that she had "overheard Cindy Fisher saying that apparently Grace Grapello's mother phoned her mother this morning to say not to bother coming by to pick up Grace because they had the ambulance people over last night because Grace was practicing her moves for **THE SOUND OF MUSIC** and she slipped and broke an ankle and now she is on crutches."

Of course this gets me thinking because there is not long till the school play performance and will her ankle be mended in time?

And if not, who will play the part of Liesl?

And guess who knows the whole part by heart?

On the way into class, I pass Karl Wrenbury, but he doesn't look at me and all day he is quiet.

And later in class, I am waiting for Mrs. Wilberton to say the news but she doesn't so in the end I am forced to ask because I absolutely have to know. I say, "Mrs. Wilberton, now that Grace Grapello has got a broken ankle and has to have crutches, who do you think will be the part of Liesl?"

Mrs. Wilberton says, "Hmm, well, that just depends on who knows the part, doesn't it?"

Then I say, "Mrs. Wilberton, I know the part."

Because you see I do, because I have been learning it like mad because Mr. Washington said if you learn things by heart, it is a good way of exercising your memory.

And then Mrs. Wilberton goes all shuffly and she says, "Well, we are not going to discuss it now since nobody knows whether Grace will be able to perform or not."

And Betty says, "But Mrs. Wilberton, it takes at least six to eight weeks to mend a broken ankle and so there won't be time for Grace to mend hers before the play and she will definitely be needing both her ankles for the part of Liesl—it is not a part you can do with just the one. Skipping is involved."

And Mrs. Wilberton says, "I will be the judge of whose ankles are or aren't right for the part, thank you very much!"

＊ ＊ ＊

Later on at home, I am in the middle of discovering that there is no **K** in **anxious** when the doorbell rings and Grandad answers it.

It's Karl Wrenbury. He's come to collect Grandad and Cement for dog training.

I hear Grandad say, "Oh, Clarice is home. Shall we get her to come too?"

And Karl says, "It's better not to have too many people—it can be very distracting for the dog if there's too much going on."

And this might be a bit true, but it's not completely true.

Can Lying Ever be Quite a Good thing?

Mr. Washington is encouraging us to write down the main events of our lives. He says it doesn't have to be the big stuff that makes interesting reading. He says sometimes the tiny everyday details of our day are what is fascinating.

Maybe he is right.

I tell him a typical morning in our family is this:

"Help! Someone's stolen my shoes."

"Minal's eaten an earwig."

"Dad, Fuzzy's fallen in the toilet."

Dad doesn't even blink at that time in the morning. He just says, "Earwigs are very nutritious."

Mr. Washington says, "Doesn't your dad's

response tell you a lot about what kind of man he is?"

I say, "Yes, he's the sort of person who does not want to fish a cat out of a toilet."

Mr. Washington says, "Yes, that's true, but he's also unflappable—he's not going to let an earwig upset him. I bet he's the kind of man who is good in an emergency."

This is true. When Grandad locked himself in the bathroom by accident, Dad was very calm about it and immediately, right away went to call Uncle Ted, who is an expert at getting people out of bathrooms.

Even though Uncle Ted couldn't get there for forty-2 or so minutes, Dad said it would all be all right because Grandad was in the best place a man with a weak bladder could be.

Dad even got the ladder out and managed to hand Grandad a few cookies through the tiny window. So you see Mr. Washington is right— Dad is not a flapper.

I write all this down because Mr. Washington has made me realize it is much more interesting than I had at first thought and might be good in a story.

I notice that Karl is not writing anything. And I am getting a bit fidgety in case Karl will do something like what happened before.

Mr. Washington says, "What's up, Karl?"

Karl says, "I am not going to write anything about my private life."

And when he says this, all the class goes quiet.

But Mr. Washington says, "No problem, Karl—so make something up. Write about the private life you wish you had. I don't know anything about you. If you told me you were from the planet Zoot, how would I know?"

Karl says, "There isn't a planet Zoot." ✻

Mr. Washington says, "See, there's another thing I didn't know. I'm learning all the time."

Karl really likes this idea and he ends up writing something really good. Later Mr. Washington reads it aloud to the whole class as an example of

---

✻ **Zoot** is not in fact a planet; however Mercury, Venus, Earth, Mars, Jupiter, Saturn, Uranus, Neptune, and Pluto are.

good writing, and I notice that Karl is trying not to look pleased but I can tell he is.

His story is all about this dog and this old man who this boy is trying to train to have manners but the old man and the dog have been hypnotized by this scary woman with glasses and feet like trotters because she is trying to take over the world by making all the dogs in the universe bark at once and cause everyone to go crazy.

It's very clever and I know at least some of it is true.

Mr. Washington asks us all these questions about Karl's story and asks us all what makes it so good and what did everyone like about it.

And Suzie Woo says, "It's clever because when there is a lot of noise like barking, you can't hear yourself think and you can't listen to anyone either and that's when you feel like you are going crazy, and if everyone went crazy you could of course take over the world."

I want to say something, but I feel

awkward now that Karl doesn't like me so I just keep my mouth shut.

Noah says he likes the character of the scary woman with trotter feet and Karl looks really pleased and he smiles slightly.

And I wish I could have been the one to say it.

❋ ❋ ❋

At home I am thinking about writing and how you can make anything up and you can also use things that really happened but make them a bit different all at the same time. So some things are real and some things are invented but who knows which?

I once saw this movie where this woman just made everything up.

Everything.

And people believed her and they liked her so it was sort of OK.

They weren't bad lies; they were funny ones.

You see, what she did was just invent things and it just made her seem more exciting.

And this man fell in love with her because she

was such an interesting person and even though she didn't do all the *interesting* things she said she did, it turns out she was still interesting because she thought up such interesting things.

Sometimes you don't get the chance to do all the things you dream of doing but that doesn't mean you aren't a fascinating person.

Surely if you can imagine yourself doing all the exciting things, then really that makes you *more* fascinating because you are using your brain to think it up.

And that is really what the movie is about, traveling in your imagination.

It's a bit like when you have a dream and you feel like you have actually done something like ride a horse even when you haven't.

So if I can tell someone what it was like when I galloped around on a horse down a mountain in Holland, where I have never been, then surely that is fascinating because I have thought it up out of nowhere.

When I get home, I see Mom is out talking to Mrs. Stampney and I overhear Mrs. Stampney saying, "Do you like my new garden statue?"

It's of a frog holding an umbrella.

And I hear Mom say, "Yes, Marjorie, it's . . . delightful."

Which I for a fact know is not the utter truth because I heard Mom say yesterday she thought it was an eyesore. And when I ask Mom why she told such a big whopper, she says because sometimes people's feelings are more important than what we really think.

I say, "So fibs are fine so long as you can come up with a good reason."

Mom says, "This does not mean that fibbing is fine, i.e., if you ate all the chocolate cookies but said it was Minal, then this is not fine."

How does she know this???

Since there *are* no cookies, I have to eat a dry piece of stale-ish bread while I watch the next installment of Ruby Redfort, called

KEEP YOUR COOL, CLANCY CREW.

What's happened is Clancy Crew has got in trouble with Mr. Parker, Ruby's next-door neighbor. Mr. Parker is lividly furious because he has caught Clancy Crew in his flower bed trampling around on his roses.

Mr. Parker doesn't know it, but Clancy is setting up a special bugging antenna aerial thing in his flower bed. It's disguised as a fly, which is really, of course, very clever. I am not quite sure what it's for because Minal was having a little bit of a tantrum about there being no cookies so I couldn't hear the TV over his whining.

Anyway, you can bet it has something to do with someone, somewhere wanting to take over the world.

Anyway, Mr. Parker is really beside himself and ready to call the cops and he is holding on to Clancy by the ear, which looks painful.

Luckily Ruby Redfort is on the scene. She pretends to be all breathless from running and she says, "Did you catch it, Clance?"
CLANCY: "UH, UMM?"
Clancy is looking at Ruby out of the corner of his eye, trying to catch her drift, his ear is still being held by Mr. Parker.

MR. PARKER: "Catch what? What's to catch?"
Mr. Parker is all baffled and not sure what is
going on.
RUBY: "Oh, hi there, Mr. Parker. Clancy saw a
giant rodent run into your rosebushes. My father says
they play havoc with roses and are always chewing
up his and just give 'em two seconds and well, you
can forget about winning the best rose award, if you
know what I'm saying. Thank goodness Clancy was
there—he practically flew over your wall when he
saw it, didn't you, Clance?"
CLANCY: "Yeah? Oh . . . uh-huh."
RUBY: "Clance just hates those giant rodents, don't
you, Clance?"
CLANCY: "Hate 'em."
All this time, Mr. Parker is just standing there
speechless.
RUBY: "Did you catch it, Clance?"
By this time Mr. Parker is utterly taken in and
believes every word of it.
MR. PARKER: "Yes, did you catch it?"
CLANCY: "I'm afraid it got into the Smithersons'
yard."

Mr. Parker hates the Smithersons so he can't help looking pleased about this.

You have to be good at acting to do this and that's the thing about Ruby Redfort—she is. And what Ruby Redfort has done is lie to Mr. Parker to cover for Clancy Crew to keep him out of trouble.

It's one of the Ruby Redfort rules: NEVER LET A GOOD PAL DOWN.

So if it's wrong if you lie to *get* someone into trouble, can it be right if you lie to *save* them from trouble?

❋ ❋ ❋

After the program, I have to do Mr. Washington's homework but I also realize I have not been **devouring**—*reading eagerly*—the dictionary lately and I will be **devastated**—*enormously upset*—if I discover that my brain is **devoid of**—*completely lacking in*—new spellings. So I have decided that I must be more **disciplined**—*have more self-control*—or I will just have to stand there in the spelling bee like a **dumbo**—*total numbskull*.

So what I decide to do is write my story for Mr. Washington while at the same time keeping an eye on the I's, i.e., I will try to include as many interesting I words in my story as I can.

I am instantly inspired by the idea about inventing things in my imagination and also including information from everyday life.

I write this story about this girl called Macy Gruber, who is an ingenious secret agent even though she is only a schoolgirl with tangly hair. She is inconspicuous and not easily noticed because she lives in a normalish family with normal parents and has a really irritating younger brother who is about fiveish. She has to share a room with him, which is a nuisance because he keeps interfering with her undercover investigations.

And he is always causing her to get in trouble and incriminates her and makes her appear guilty even though she is never involved.

Macy Gruber's grandad is always getting incarcerated and locked into the smallest room in the house, i.e., the bathroom.

Macy Gruber's sister is mainly quite rude and on the phone to France quite a lot. Macy Gruber has an older brother who works in a shop called Aubergine, selling health food, but you would never guess it but it's not really a shop at all—it is in fact incognito and disguised because really it is the secret-agent headquarters. And the shop owner, named Waldorf Parker, is in charge of the whole operation.

Of course Macy Gruber has an utterly exciting life style—as you would expect.

It takes me ages to write because I have to keep looking up words in the dictionary.

But I am quite pleased with my story, as it is very inventive.

Though trying to squeeze in so many **I**'s has made some bits a little **incoherent**—*not clearly thought out and consequently difficult to understand.*

I wonder what Mr. Washington will think.

Sometimes things are Easier if you Don't Say what you Think

Guess what? I have got the part of Liesl!

What happened was, Mrs. Wilberton came up to me all as if it was her idea in the first place and says, "I have decided that you can play the part of Liesl von Trapp, but there will be no more cheekiness. Any bad behavior and you're out—do you understand?"

Of course I say, "Yes, Mrs. Wilberton," even though I do not agree with what she has said and it is not fair because I have not been cheeky and nor have I been up to any bad behavior.

But I remember Ruby Redfort's rule of DON'T ARGUE WITH PEOPLE WHO ARE ABOUT TO GIVE YOU WHAT YOU WANT. LET THEM THINK THEY ARE IN CHARGE.

This is something Ruby Redfort herself is not good at—she always argues.

At break time, Mr. Pickering says that he is so impressed by Karl's good piece of writing in Mr. Washington's class and new effort of being less badly behaved that he can have his job back—doing the sound effects in the school play. Karl is really pleased because whatever he said about not caring was not really actually true.

And he did care actually quite a lot because he had gone to a lot of trouble collecting up sounds and fitting them in the right places.

Not that he says anything about it to me—in fact, he doesn't say anything to me at all.

We have to do rehearsals at lunchtime and it's quite fun because finally I have something to say. And I can remember it all.

My cousin Noah is playing the part of Rolf now, which is fine because I don't mind holding his hand because at least I know where it has been, i.e., not up his nose.

Thank goodness Rolf isn't Robert Granger or Toby Hawkling. Robert Granger is clomping around the stage and I must say he does not look one bit how anyone would imagine Captain von Trapp to look, although he is a surprisingly good singer.

And his singing is a much nicer noise than his talking.

We have to wear our costumes—which means it is called a "dress rehearsal." *

And Suzie Woo has forgotten her Maria apron and so she has to borrow one from Mrs. Ooseman the lunch lady and it has apple brown Betty on it.

When she comes on, Karl does a really good sound of the wind blowing because at the beginning she is meant to be up a mountain. And when Mrs. Wilberton walks onto the stage to tell Alexandra Holker to stop chattering, Karl does a slightly different windy sound, which is rude.

And Mrs. Wilberton says, "Karl, what was that noise?"

And Karl says, "Sorry, Mrs. Wilberton—it went off by accident."

And Mrs. Wilberton is so astonished to hear

---

* **Dress rehearsal**—performing the whole play in your costume and everything but with no audience.

Karl say sorry that she forgets to tell him off.

And even though everyone knows he did it on purpose to be funny, he has gotten out of trouble by using the simplest Ruby Redfort rule: SOMETIMES IT IS SMART TO SAY SORRY EVEN WHEN YOU ARE NOT.

I am quite excited about my outfit. Mom has made it for me and it is really fairly twirly and I spend most of my time twirling.

I am still hoping my Ruby Redfort fly hair clip arrives this week since I would really like to wear it for the play. I have decided Liesl is the sort of girl who would wear a Ruby Redfort hair clip.

Czarina says it is good to put some of your own personality into a character you are playing. So this is my own idea of what Liesl is like.

❋ ❋ ❋

At the pegs after school, I bump into Karl Wrenbury getting his coat. He sort of looks at me and I think he even might say something but then Toby Hawkling comes barging along and starts

giving Karl a Chinese burn and then they start
wrestling about on the floor,

so I go off to find Betty.

* * *

We, me and Betty, are walking to drama
workshop and we are all extremely excited as we
only have one week to go before the performance
and I hope I do not forget any of my lines and
end up standing there like a lemon.

A non-speaking lemon.

Czarina has said sometimes people do
forget their lines but it is all due to nerves.

And then, there suddenly is Mrs.
Stampney. She tuts at us because me and
Betty are sharing a package of jellybeans.
I offer her one and she says, "They'll rot your
teeth, you know," and I want to say, "At least I've
got teeth to rot." But I don't, because Mom would
say, "That's rude and however rude Mrs. Stampney
is to you, there's no need to sink to her level."

At drama workshop, Czarina says we will be

non-
speaking
lemon

doing some improvising, which just means making it up as you go along and whatever might have happened to you for instance today, is something that you can use and turn into drama.

Me and Betty do a drama about an old witch who tries to steal young children's teeth.

Czarina says it is full of depth and is an interesting allegory about adults spoiling childhood dreams. I am not sure what allegory means and neither is Betty. But when Mol comes to pick us up, she says, "It can be a story that tells you two things at the same time—the actual story and then also an underlying slightly disguised message."

We are obviously much more clever than I thought we were.

And it's the sort of thing Ruby Redfort might use, a story that she could say in public which had a secret meaning to it so only Clancy Crew would understand.

We tell Mol how in drama workshop Czarina has been talking about how it is important to watch the way other people act. This is one good way of learning the craft.

I say I think we might need to watch much more television, although Mol says, "Perhaps Czarina means that you should observe how people behave in their everyday life."

She might be right, but just to be on the safe side, as soon as I get home I turn on the TV.

And it is an episode of Ruby Redfort called

HERE'S LOOKING AT YOU, KID.

I've seen it before. It's not that good.

It's the one where Ruby discovers that the evil Count von Viscount has got hold of these special x-ray glasses and is reading everyone's secret documents and mail without taking them out of the envelopes. He wants to take over the world, of course.

It's a bit far-fetched but I am still utterly on the edge of my seat. Unfortunately, just at the good part, Mom says, "Clarice, you wouldn't like to nip down to Eggplant for me, would you?"

Waldo Park called to say Mom has accidentally left the groceries behind. She has forgotten them because Minal was distracting her by having a tantrum, which Mom said was utterly embarrassing.

She said to him, "Next time you do that, I'm going to do it too and see how you like it."

And the answer is no, I do not want to go to Eggplant and miss my program.

But then, it's not really a question.

So I go.

✺ ✺ ✺

On the way, I have to walk past the park and I can see Grandad and Cement being trained by Karl. He has really improved them, and it is amazing how well behaved they are with him. Something good has rubbed off.

It's a bit like with Karl and Mr. Washington.

When they spot me, Grandad waves and Cement barks—but only once because he can see Karl doing his special no-barking signal.

And I am waiting for Karl to do his Mrs.-Wilberton-with-trotters impression.

But he never does.

Sometimes you find yourself Doing Things you wouldn't Expect Yourself to do

17

When I get to school, I see that surprisingly the builder people have gone at last and I can get around the back and finally rescue my Ruby notebook, which I dropped over the wall the other week.

I am frantic about it because it has all my secret notes in it. And I am thinking thank goodness there has been a drought and it has not rained or it would have been ruined. And thank goodness it has a padlock on it or someone could have read all my private things.

When I get around the corner, I see all the building stuff has been moved and they have finished mending whatever they were mending and I can see my Ruby notebook still lying there on the ground. But I also see something else.

It's all this writing in red spray-paint all over the wall. And it says in really big letters

SCHOOL STINKS

and then quite a very rude thing about Mrs. Wilberton. Which I know she will not be happy about.

And I notice something that makes me think— you see, one of the spellings is wrong.

There is no **H** in the word rhinoceros.

And right away I just know who wrote it and of course he will be absolutely chucked out of the school and there will be no more second chances. Because this is what's called **vandalism**—*willful*

destruction of property, i.e., ruining something
utterly on purpose.

And it is a very serious thing and you can get in
big trouble for it, especially if you write a very
rude thing about Mrs. Wilberton.

And I am just staring at the words,
and I keep thinking I know about the secret **H**
and I hope this word comes up in the spelling bee
because people will be really impressed that I
know how to spell **rhinoceros,** because **rhinoceros**
is a tricky spelling.

Then I see the spray can. It has rolled under one
of the benches and of course that would explain
the weird hissing noise that I heard when I was
walking past the school on the way back from
Betty's.

And I bend down and reach under the bench
and pick it up.

It is almost empty and I shake it a bit and a bit of
red comes off on my hand—and then suddenly the
bell rings and I quickly run into class so I won't get
told off by Mrs. Wilberton for being late.

Everyone is chatting like mad because the school

play is next week, which is exciting, and even though we still have to do this stupid spelling bee on Tuesday, after that it will be vacation.

Everyone all of a sudden looks up because there is a loud clunk of the door being flung open and Mrs. Wilberton comes storming into the classroom like she is almost not in touch with the floor.

And Mrs. Wilberton says in this really deep low voice that is almost not humanish,

"This is the LAST straw
    that broke the camel's back.
I have had it up to here.
    I have been STRETCHED
    to my very limits and back again.
      I can take NO more.
This is it, the final insult.
Who, may I ask, is the owner of
      this notebook?"

And high up in her hand she is holding this Ruby Redfort notebook.

And I think, I wonder why Mrs. Wilberton

would have a Ruby Redfort notebook. It looks just like my Ruby Redfort notebook—it has a padlock and everything.

And then I realize it *is* my Ruby Redfort notebook and I must have forgotten to pick it up.

Then Mrs. Wilberton says,

"Well, if no one knows
WHO this notebook belongs to,
then perhaps someone does know
WHO wrote that
disgraceful graffiti on the back
of the school wall."

And she is staring down at Karl and he is staring up at her and his eyes are not blinking and his mouth isn't opening. It is closed tight.

And I am feeling panicky because nothing is happening and no one is saying anything and it sort of goes on for minutes but I think it is only seconds.

And Mrs. Wilberton says,

"Well, whoever did write
that dreadful graffiti certainly can't SPELL
the word rhinoceros."

And I look at Karl,
    and he looks at me.
And suddenly Mrs. Wilberton is staring
    at my hand,
        because somehow it is in the air.
And then I hear myself say,
        "I did it."
And Mrs. Wilberton slams my Ruby Redfort
notebook down on her desk and says,

"I see, Clarice Bean,
that YOU have been caught,
        as it were, red-handed"
and I look at my hand and it's true—it is all red,
so *anyone* would think it was me.
    And Mrs. Wilberton says,

"Well, I must say I AM surprised.
I would have expected this sort of
        disgraceful graffiti to be
the work of Karl Wrenbury.
However, what does NOT astonish me
    is that you can't spell the word
        RHINOCEROS."

Out of the corner of my eye, I can see Karl and his eyes are all huge and he is trying to catch my attention but I won't look at him.

And Mrs. Wilberton says,

"RIGHT, young lady.
You can be sure your parents are going
to hear about this and
you can forget about playing Liesl
in the school play.
In fact you can FORGET about
the school play altogether."

Of course this is only to be expected. If you own up to a bad thing that you in fact didn't even do, you might as well expect your life to be ruined.

Because that is just what seems to happen.

※ ※ ※

Of course I have to go straight to Mr. Pickering's office to explain myself, which of course
I can't because I have no idea why I would
do it since I didn't do it.

This makes Mr. Pickering much more upset.

He says, "Do you really hate school?"

And I feel bad because he looks sort of sad but all I do is shrug.

And he says, "I thought you would feel able to come and tell me if something was wrong."

But I say nothing.

And he says, "I am very disappointed in you, Clarice Bean. It is not a nice thing to write unkind things about people and it is not nice to paint graffiti on school property when there are people trying to keep this school looking nice. I will have to arrange with Mr. Skippard for you to come back during vacation and clean it all up."

Then he just shakes his head and says, "I have phoned your parents and you are to go straight home. I have got nothing more to say."

And he doesn't even look up or say goodbye or anything. He just starts marking some pieces of paper.

And of course I want to say "But it wasn't me, Mr. Pickering" but I know this would be bad because what would happen to Karl?

And now that things are going much better for him, it would be worse for him to be chucked out.

So I keep my trap shut like everyone has been telling me I should.

I just wish I had kept it shut half an hour ago.

But it's like Ruby Redfort always says:

"Sometimes you just gotta do what you gotta do."

And I'm thinking about that on my way out of school, so I nip around the back and I pick up the spray can and I really don't know why I do it but I just can't help myself.

And what I do is I add an **h** into the word **rhinoceros**.

And then I just look at it and feel happy that I can spell this word.

Finally there is a word I can remember how to spell.

And it's like Ruby Redfort would say:

"Sometimes you just gotta be right about something."

❋ ❋ ❋

I get home and Mom and Dad are sitting there and they are all quiet.

I don't like it when they are quiet because this means they are really mad—not just a bit mad but really fed up. It's even worse than that because Mom is also upset and worried.

I know this because it is written all over her face.

She says, "Clarice, this was not a good thing to do. I thought we had taught you better than this."

Dad says nothing at all.

I say nothing at all.

Mom says, "What were you thinking?"

I shrug because genuinely I do not know.

Mom says, "I am struggling for words."

I can't think of any myself.

Then she says, "This is more like the kind of thing Karl Wrenbury would do."

I look a bit sheepish because as I have told you before, my mom is good at mind reading.

I take a deep breath and wait for her to see that I have told a big fib.

But amazingly she doesn't.

It must be because I have become such a good actor and I am so good at looking guilty and like someone who would do graffiti that she can't help being fooled.

She just says, "Your father and I were so looking forward to seeing you in the school play. I know how much you wanted to act and now you have thrown away the chance."

I don't say a word because as Ruby Redfort would say, "Sometimes you just gotta know when to keep it buttoned."

Sometimes you just have to Let people be Mad until they Stop Being Mad

I am missing the last week of school as a punishment. I have to go back to school the next day though to collect all my stuff for summer vacation.

Mom comes with me but she waits in the playground. I don't want her to come into the school.

The first person I have to go and bump into is Robert Granger.

He says, "Hello, Clarice Bean. It's a real shame you got in trouble and aren't allowed to be in **THE SOUND OF MUSIC** because you had one of the main parts and I thought you were really good and it's going to be a really good play."

I say, "I doubt that, Robert Granger.

THE SOUND OF MUSIC is for drips."

And I don't let him see that I am utterly disappointed and I am missing something that was the thing I most was looking forward to.

What's true is, at least I will not have to be in the stupid spelling bee.

I can't help thinking that it's kind of funny that the only tricky word that I managed to learn how to spell has ended up getting me in some very big trouble.

Because if I hadn't known how to spell the word *rhinoceros* then I wouldn't have known that Karl Wrenbury *didn't*.

And then I would never have known he was the one who wrote it on the wall.

And if I hadn't known it was him who was going to get in trouble, then I would not have stood up for him.

And if I hadn't stood up for him, I would not be in big trouble myself now.

It just goes to prove what I always thought—that spelling just causes all kinds of problems for people.

I have to go and collect my summer vacation work from Mrs. Wilberton and she is just as you would expect.

Not exactly nice.

Then I go to see Mr. Washington, to say goodbye. He is going back to Trinidad. He is sitting on his desk reading something.

He looks up when I go in and says, "Hello, **CB**. How are you doing today?"

He says it just like nothing at all has ever happened.

I say, "You know . . . OK" and I sort of shrug because things are not OK.

And he says, "Yeah, I know." Then he says, "Well, what I really wanted to say to you is I have read your story and I think it really is very good. You seem to manage to get people just perfectly, almost as if you have taken notes and written down exactly what they say. I reckon you are going to become an excellent writer one day."

And I say, "But Mr. Washington, I can't even *spell* the word excellent. How can I be an *excellent* writer if I can't *spell* excellent?"

And Mr. Washington says, "Spelling is not what makes you a writer. Having something interesting to say is what counts, and you know what? You are someone who always has something interesting to say and also, **CB**, all that studying has paid off—you have a wonderful vocabulary."

Then he pats me on the back and says, "This will all blow over—just have a good summer."

I say, "Mr. Washington, I think you are a really good teacher and so does Betty Moody and I have really enjoyed your lessons and I have learned a lot and have a good summer too."

And he says, "That means a lot, **CB**, and is exceptionordinarily nice of you to say so."

And we say goodbye and I go to get all my things out of my locker. And when I get to my locker, there is Karl—he's been waiting for me.

I say, "You are supposed to be in class—you will get in trouble."

He shrugs and says, "Thanks for not telling on me. Sorry I wasn't talking to you and for saying you weren't my friend."

And I say, "Don't mention it, kid," because I

know that's exactly what Ruby Redfort
would say.

trotters

And then he runs off down the corridor, and
when he gets to Mrs. Wilberton's classroom,
he does this impression of walking on trotters
and then he's gone.

I close my locker and I go too.

❋ ❋ ❋

I am not allowed to see Betty Moody for one
actual week but Mom says I may talk to her on
the telephone. So, later, I give her a call and she
tells me how Grace Grapello won the spelling bee.

She says she thinks Grace was given all the easy
words because everyone felt sorry for her because
she was on crutches.

I say, "It wouldn't surprise me."

Betty says, "It was obvious that Karl Wrenbury
should have won it because he knew how to
spell **onomatopoeia**. ❋ And who knows how
to spell that?"

❋ **Onomatopoeia** (sounds like *on-a-matta-pee-uh*) means a word that
sounds like its meaning, i.e., *whoosh, buzz, ping*.

I say, "Yes, it sounds a bit like a caterpillar."

Then Betty says, "By the way, I know you didn't do it, Clarice Bean, and that was really nice of you not to tell on Karl and he said no one has stuck up for him before."

I say, "But Ruby Redfort would never ever tell on Clancy Crew. I was only doing what Ruby herself would do."

And Betty Moody says, "You're right there, **CB**."

Some things are Hard to Believe Even when they are Utterly True

I am not allowed to go to the school play because I am in disgrace. I am meant to mooch around at home and think about what I have done and try not to enjoy myself.

Mom is feeling a bit sorry for me. Dad is feeling a bit sorry for himself because he had hoped to get out of work early and come and see me act but now he has no excuse.

One nice thing that has happened today is finally my Ruby Redfort fly hair clip has arrived. I do really like it and it was worth the $1.99 plus six spaghetti tokens but it isn't enough to make me feel utterly better.

But I slide it in my hair anyway.

Then Mom knocks on my door and says, "Kurt called. He was wondering if you could nip down to Eggplant because he needs his spare T-shirt."

I am surprised he has asked me to go and it's strange because it is not his normal day for working at Eggplant and I am pleased that Mom is letting me go out.

So I ask her if it would be all right to also get an herbal juice—nothing too tasty.

She says, "I think you have suffered enough, get a Popsicle."

She gives me a dollar fifty. I will probably get a strawberry one or maybe banana, I have gone off mango.

I am thinking about this as I walk down the street and I am looking at the pavement.

I am thinking about all the chewing gum which is stuck to the paving slabs and how it will probably never come off and that it's a shame that people don't just put it in the trash because it would look nicer if they did.

And I am thinking about this and about all

the ants who live in the cracks and what do *they* think of the chewing gum.

And I am thinking of everyone at school and how they will be just about to start the school play and how I was going to be in it, and also how I was going to be one of the starring people, and how now I will never ever most likely be spotted by one of those talent spotter people, and I will never become a child star like Skyler Summer. And how I will never be famous on TV.

And I am thinking about this so much that when I look up from looking at the sidewalk I am actually at Eggplant.

And what's strange is, there are all these people standing around outside and there are lots of lights and equipment things. And I can see Waldo Park—he is standing on the curb with my brother and Kira, so I wriggle through to where they are and I say, "Hey, what's going on?"

And guess what Waldo Park says?

"It's Hollywood, baby."

And although Waldo says it in this joking voice, guess what? He isn't joking. It really is the movie people right here in Sesame Park Road. And they *are* the people from **HOLLYWOOD**.

I say, "What are they doing a movie of?"

And Waldo Park is just about to say when I hear this voice behind me.

And then the voice says,

"Hey, kid, you a Ruby Redfort fan?"

And I say, "How do you know?"

And the man taps my fly hair clip and says,

"Looking good, kid,"

and I say, "Whadda ya know" which is something Ruby Redfort herself would say— because guess who I am talking to? Only Ruby's butler, Hitch.

But it's not actually Hitch, of course. It's the actor of Hitch, George Conway.

I say, "Wow, are you filming the Ruby Redfort Hollywood movie here in Sesame Park Road? I live on this street almost and my brother works in this shop, Eggplant, and I come here all the time nearly. Wow, I can't believe it."

And you see I can't stop talking—a bit like in

this one episode of Ruby Redfort when Clancy Crew has accidentally drunk a truth potion and he can't stop babbling. And that's what I am doing, babbling.

Then one of the Hollywood people comes up to Kurt and says,

"Hey, is this your sister who you were telling us about? Just what we're looking for, a kid to walk into the shop—do you feel happy acting?"

And I say, "What?"

And then George Conway says,

"Kid, do you wanna be in the picture?"

And I can't even talk because I am astonished and astoundingly amazed and so I stand there not speaking. The one time I need to say something and I can't open my mouth.

But then my brother Kurt says, "Yes she wants to be in the picture."

And I look at Kurt and he winks at me. And the Hollywood people say, **"super."**

And then I have my makeup done in the trailer, and I don't have to wear a costume or anything because I am meant to look like a real person because that's my part.

Then who comes in but Skyler Summer and the makeup lady instantly starts brushing her hair like mad and no wonder she has such neat hair because who wouldn't if someone brushed it nonstop.

And then Skyler Summer says,

"Oh my gosh, I've lost my Ruby fly hair clip,"

and they all start looking for it and I say,

"I've got one you can have,"

and Skyler Summer says,

"Hey, like thanks a whole lot."

And I say, "No problemo" because I really don't mind because even though I didn't get to wear my fly hair clip in the school play, it means the actual Ruby Redfort actress will wear my fly clip in the actual Hollywood movie.

Though of course it does mean I will have to start eating spaghetti again.

When I go outside, the Hollywood people
tell me what I have to do. And one of the
Hollywood people says,

"SCENE 6, TAKE 1, ACTION."

And I have to walk into the shop and pretend
to buy a Popsicle and then walk out and then
the Hitch actor reaches out and grabs my
Popsicle and skids it along the pavement, and
then the actor playing the evil villain Hogtrotter
has to slip on the Popsicle
and then Skyler Summer, who is being Ruby
Redfort herself, jumps out of the car and sits on
him so he can't escape.

And then she goes, "Looks like you really
slipped up this time, Hogtrotter, my old fiend."

And then she turns to me and says, "Thanks a
lot, kid" and taps the fly hair clip.

And then the Hollywood person goes,

"CUT."

And you see, all I had to do is look surprised, which is reacting of course and I know how to do this because Czarina taught us this in drama workshop—so although this is a really difficult thing to do, it's easy for me because I have had the training.

It is all utterly exciting and I do it in one take, as they say in the movie business.

And when I have finished, George Conway gives me a squeeze on the cheek and says,

"You did good, kid."

Which is of course exactly the kind of thing Hitch would say.

❋ ❋ ❋

And I know you might not believe me, but it's all absolutely true.

Some days strange things happen. And you may

think you are just going off to buy a Popsicle but then you are suprised to find you are actually talking to Ruby Redfort herself.

You see, sometimes things are hard to explain.

Sometimes things that go wrong also go right.

And sometimes your bad luck just has to turn good.

This book is for the
exceptionordinarily super

Alex and *Jenny*

love, Lauren P.
You better believe it, buster.

Hey, like thanks a whole lot to

Waldo Park

and his super shop, Sesame.

Super thanks to

*Ann-Janine Murtagh, Goldy Broad,
Ruth Alltimes, Cressida Cowell,
Jenny Valentine, and
Pat and Chris Cutforth.*

Glad you could make it, kids.

Don't miss these other exceptionordinarily good books about Clarice Bean!

Utterly Me, Clarice Bean

Hardcover ISBN 978-0-7636-2186-5
Paperback ISBN 978-0-7636-2788-1

Clarice Bean, Don't Look Now

Hardcover ISBN 978-0-7636-3536-7
Paperback ISBN 978-0-7636-3935-8

CLARICE BEAN'S FAVORITE CHARACTER HAS A BOOK OF HER OWN!

Ruby Redfort is coming your way soon!

Here is what Clarice Bean has to say about this new series: "The thing I love about the Ruby Redfort series is that it is always exciting and quite impossible to imagine how Ruby will get out of the death-defying situation she is in. Mostly I spend the whole time behind a chair or grabbing a cushion. If you like death-defying situations and gadgets and a girl who is more tough then an archish villian then you will love Ruby Redfort."

www.rubyredfort.com
www.candlewick.com